“Do you want to teach your daughter a lesson?”

Courtney cocked her head in Graham’s direction. “Because you know the best way to do that would be to beat Rachel at her own game.”

“I’m not sure what you mean,” Graham admitted.

“I think we’ve both figured out the reason I’m here is because Rachel thought if we hit it off, you’d be willing to move back to New York City.”

He snorted. “Not likely to happen.”

“So what if we let Rachel think her idea worked when she gets home? Except instead of you going to New York, we’ll tell her I’ve decided to move to Alaska?”

He threw his head back and laughed. “To quote Rachel’s favorite expression, she would totally freak out.”

“Exactly,” Courtney said with a smile.

Dear Reader,

Like many authors, I also have a day job. One of the things I enjoy about being a dental hygienist is meeting interesting people.

Recently one of my patients married a man she'd met on an online dating site. The venue she used to meet her Mr. Right wasn't what intrigued me. What intrigued me was that this man lived in a remote part of Alaska.

I thought of the drastic changes she and her teenage daughter would face living in such a secluded place, especially from her daughter's point of view. Can you imagine telling a teenager she would be living with no shopping malls, no movie theaters, no fast-food and—*gasp*—no cell phone service?

That's when my inspiration for *Dad's E-mail Order Bride* was born. I decided to tell my story from a different angle. Fifteen-year-old Rachel Morrison isn't going to Alaska—she's there with her stubborn widower dad who has no interest in moving back to New York City. Rachel's goal: pretend to be her dad on an online dating site and find him a wife from New York so he'll have a reason to return to civilization.

Getting to know my characters in this book was great fun for me. I hope you enjoy reading it as much as I enjoyed writing it.

Cheers,

Candy Halliday

Dad's E-mail Order Bride

Candy Halliday

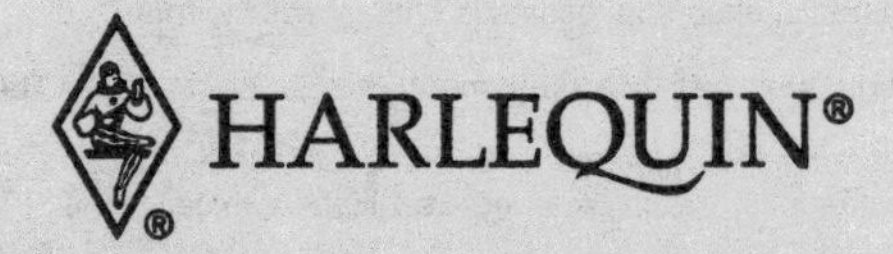

TORONTO • NEW YORK • LONDON
AMSTERDAM • PARIS • SYDNEY • HAMBURG
STOCKHOLM • ATHENS • TOKYO • MILAN • MADRID
PRAGUE • WARSAW • BUDAPEST • AUCKLAND

Recycling programs
for this product may
not exist in your area.

ISBN-13: 978-0-373-71629-6

DAD'S E-MAIL ORDER BRIDE

This edition published by arrangement with Harlequin Books S.A.

For questions and comments about the quality of this book please contact us at Customer_eCare@Harlequin.ca.

www.eHarlequin.com

Printed in U.S.A.

ABOUT THE AUTHOR

Multipublished romance author Candy Halliday lives in the Piedmont of North Carolina with her husband, a spastic schnauzer named Millie and an impossible attack cat named Flash. Candy's daughter and son-in-law and her two teenage grandchildren live nearby. Candy loves to hear from readers. Drop her a line at www.candyhalliday.com.

Books by Candy Halliday

HARLEQUIN SUPERROMANCE

1575—A RANCH CALLED HOME

This book is dedicated to the greatest group of dads I know: Tracy Cottingham, Eddie Clark, Chris Patrick, Steve Poe, Matt Miller, John Mathews, Mark Thomas, Mike Simmons and Jon Scott.

ACKNOWLEDGMENTS

Thanks always to my super agent Jenny Bent, and a huge congratulations to Jenny for launching her own literary agency: The Bent Agency.

Immense thanks to my amazing editor, Wanda Ottewell, who has incredible insight and demands the best from me.

All of my love forever to my wonderful family: Blue, Shelli, Tracy, Quint and Caroline.

CHAPTER ONE

GRAHAM MORRISON heard the noisy motor long before the floatplane came into view. He stuck his ax into the top of the log he'd been splitting with a loud *thwack*, removed his gloves and watched the plane circle the cove and make a graceful landing on the water.

Like other homes and establishments in Port Protection, Alaska, the small community was accessible only by boat, or by floatplane. Most people would have found the extreme isolation on the northern tip of Prince of Wales Island unbearable. But never once had Graham regretted coming to Alaska to renovate the fishing lodge his grandfather had left him.

Port Protection was a safe haven.

For him—and for the daughter he was raising alone.

Graham shoved his gloves into the back pocket of his jeans and started down the path to the long dock stretching out below Trail's End Lodge. His place was always the last stop for the bush pilot on Friday, but today Graham hoped Gil Hargraves wouldn't try to amuse him with any of his escapades.

Women were always Gil's favorite subject. And Gil never missed an opportunity to remind Graham what he was missing staying secluded in Port Protection where the population was less than one hundred people and where the only single woman in town was in her late seventies and had outlived three husbands.

On Gil's last trip he'd supposedly been gearing up for an amorous weekend with twin sisters from Anchorage. Other men might enjoy hearing Gil brag about his conquests, but Graham didn't.

Gil was thirty.

He needed to grow up.

The floatplane came to a stop alongside the dock. Gil switched off the loud engine, opened the door and swung himself easily out of the plane. Even Graham could understand why he didn't have a problem with the ladies. Gil was better looking than most guys, kept in shape, and Graham had heard his fifteen-year-old daughter refer to Gil more than once as *wickedly hot.*

His daughter referring to any male as *hot*—wickedly or otherwise—always made Graham cringe. Graham prayed Rachel would stay away from guys like Gil who liked to kiss and tell before moving on to the next woman.

"You're looking good, Graham," Gil said as he bent down to secure the plane's tie lead to the dock. He straightened with a menacing smirk on his face. "In fact, you don't look a day over forty."

"Don't push it, Gil," Graham warned. "I won't turn forty until tomorrow. I'm holding on to thirty-nine as long as I can."

"Well, I brought you one hell of a birthday present," Gil said, "that's for sure."

"Yeah?" Graham assumed Gil was referring to the log splitter he'd finally decided to buy rather than continue splitting wood the hard way. This birthday served to remind him he wasn't getting any younger. So he'd circled the splitter in the outdoorsman catalog, and he'd left his credit card in plain view for his daughter's benefit.

Rachel had obviously taken the hint and made the purchase on the Internet the way they did their big-item shopping. Her last words before she left for school were to remind him to stay near the lodge so he wouldn't miss Gil when the plane landed with his birthday present.

"Need any help?" Graham quizzed, offering to assist Gil in unloading.

Gil laughed. "No, but you probably will."

Graham was puzzled by his answer. And he was even more confused when Gil walked back to the plane and opened the passenger side door. There were no fishing parties scheduled for the weekend—a promise he'd made to Rachel—even though May was a peak month for salmon.

Whether Graham liked it or not, his daughter was throwing him a big party on Saturday. And Rachel had been so proud of herself for making the arrangements he hadn't had the heart to disappoint her.

But what the…?

A tall blonde stepped from the plane.

Skintight jeans tucked into high-heeled boots.

Legs that went on forever.

Gil winked at Graham when he reached for her hand. And Graham went from confused to downright stunned. She could have been a model on the cover of a fashion magazine. And now she was walking in his direction.

Graham didn't say a word when she came to a stop in front of him. Her high heels brought them almost nose-to-nose, and her eyes were as blue as the fur-trimmed parka she was wearing.

She leaned forward and kissed him gently on the lips.

Graham was tempted to kiss her again.

Until she said, "Happy. Birthday. Graham."

Her words were so stilted and robotic Graham took a quick step backward. And when he looked past her, Gil was standing at the rear of the plane grinning from ear to ear.

Just last month Gil had told him about a Russian hooker he'd met in Nome who could barely speak English. And he'd bragged he could fix Graham up with her on a moment's notice.

So the joke was on him.

Gil had paid the hooker to kiss him for his birthday.

Graham was prepared to be a good sport and laugh the whole thing off—until Gil unloaded two matching pink suitcases and placed them on the dock.

"Hey!" Graham called out in a panic and hurried in Gil's direction.

It would be just like Gil to take the joke too far—to pay the blonde to give him more than just a birthday kiss. But damn! Had Gil forgotten there was an impressionable teenage daughter to consider?

Graham made it to the plane just as Gil was reaching out to close the cargo bay door. He grabbed Gil by the arm to keep that from happening.

"Okay, Gil, the joke's over," Graham told him. "You seem to have forgotten I have a daughter. So pick up the luggage, get your friend back into the plane and—"

"Whoa!" Gil said, jerking his arm away. "She isn't any friend of mine. I've never seen her before."

"This isn't funny," Graham warned.

Gil looked past him for a second. "Your guest doesn't seem to think this is funny, either."

Graham glanced over his shoulder.

The frown on her face sent a shiver up his spine.

"Wait right here," he told Gill.

Gil shook his head. "No way. I have a hot date with a redhead in Ketchikan tonight and I'm already behind schedule. The blonde is your problem. I'll be back to pick her up on Monday when I drop off your guests for next week."

Graham took a threatening step forward. "Don't be a wiseass, Gil. I have no idea who this woman is. And she certainly can't stay here all weekend."

Gil peered around him again. "Don't you be a *dumb* ass, Graham. Whoever she is, she's a knockout, man. And you've got a big lodge with a bunch of empty rooms for her to choose from. If you don't know her, get to know her. That's what I'd do."

"I'm not you," Graham said between clenched teeth.

"Your loss," Gil said and bent down to unfasten the tie lead.

"I mean it, Gil," Graham said. "Don't you leave this dock until I get this straightened out."

Graham turned and walked in the blonde's direction. He was midway to where she stood when the sound of the noisy engine coming back to life jerked Graham's head around.

"Dammit, Gil!"

Gil's reply was a final salute before he sped across the cove. Two seconds later the only chance Graham had of his birthday present leaving before Monday lifted into the air. Two seconds more and the plane flew around the cove and disappeared out of sight.

Graham looked over his shoulder again. Now she had her hands on her hips. And she didn't look one bit happy.

That made two of them.

WHEN THE FLOATPLANE left without her, the first thought that crossed Courtney Woods's mind was to jump off the dock and start swimming to the mainland. And she might have done just that had she not been so upset with the man walking up the dock in her direction.

She obviously didn't measure up to Graham Morrison's standards. She'd seen the shocked look on his face the second she stepped off the plane.

But did she really look so different in person than she did in her pictures? Or was Graham one of those guys who only got into the fantasy part of an online relationship? Now that she was actually standing on his dock in the flesh, all of the interest was gone.

But why send her the airplane ticket?

Why invite her to his birthday party tomorrow?

Why lie to her on so many different levels?

What a disaster!

Had her best friend Beth not given her a membership to an online dating service for her birthday as a joke, Courtney never would have known about a Web site called LoveFromAlaska.com. And she certainly wouldn't have been suckered by the man walking toward her now, who had obviously changed his mind.

But turning thirty-five had hit her like the big wrecking ball she'd used in one of her most successful ad campaigns. And the catchy slogan she'd come up with for the career placement service had been: "Break out of your going-nowhere life."

For once, Courtney had taken her own advice.

And what had it gotten her? A trip all the way across country only to be rejected by the very man who had invited her to come.

Still, Courtney thought, *what a shame.*

She'd been so sure Graham Morrison was the real thing.

He stopped in front of her. And as luck would have it, he was even *better* looking in person. Thick, black hair. Rock-hard body. Dark brown eyes she could easily get lost in.

He cleared his throat and said, "There's obviously been some mistake here."

"You think?" Courtney shot back.

He seemed surprised by her sarcasm.

"It's also obvious you can hear every word I'm saying," Courtney said. "Why would you lie about something so serious, Graham? Why would you say you lost your hearing in an explosion while you were clearing land for the lodge?"

"What?" he bellowed back at her.

Courtney's eyes narrowed. "Well, isn't this convenient? You miraculously have your hearing back, but now you've lost your memory!"

"Now, look here," he began.

"No, you look here," Courtney told him. "Are you really going to stand there and pretend we haven't been corresponding on the Internet since February? That you didn't invite me to your birthday party tomorrow? And that you didn't pay for my airplane ticket to get here?"

Before he could answer, Courtney dug into her purse and pulled out the card that had finally made her decide to come to Alaska.

Don't you think it's time we met? Say yes, and come to my birthday party.
Love from Alaska, Graham.

Courtney shoved the card into his hands. "I guess you also didn't send me this card when you mailed me the itinerary for my e-ticket."

He frowned. "This is my daughter's handwriting."

"Rachel wrote that?"

Now he looked concerned. "How do you know Rachel?"

Courtney snatched the card back. "You know perfectly well how I know Rachel. She calls me every night."

Or did he know that?

The thought made Courtney gasp.

He kept staring at her.

And Courtney said, "You really don't know who I am, do you?"

"No," he said. "Who are you?"

Courtney needed to sit down.

But there was nowhere to sit!

"I'm Courtney Woods," she finally told him. "The idiot who's been corresponding with your daughter pretending to be you."

His expression said he'd figured that out already.

He headed down the dock for her suitcases. When he returned, he said, "I'm sorry, but that was—"

"The last flight out of here until Monday," Courtney finished for him.

He nodded.

"And there aren't any hotels in Port Protection."

"No," he confirmed, "there aren't."

"So, basically I guess that means—"

"It means you can stay at the lodge until Monday."

He'd saved her from saying "you're stuck with me."

But they both knew that's what he was thinking.

He motioned toward the path leading to the lodge. "Let's go inside," he said. "I'll make some coffee while we sort this out."

Lace my cup with strychnine, Courtney prayed. All she wanted to do was curl into a ball and *die!*

CHAPTER TWO

GRAHAM TOOK THEIR coffee cups to the kitchen for a refill, trying to process everything Courtney had told him so far. She said Rachel had contacted her on an online dating Web site. And the minute Courtney said she was an advertising executive from New York City, Graham knew exactly why Courtney was the one Rachel had picked.

Rachel had been furious with him for months now because he refused to let her return to New York to finish high school. She'd even dragged his parents and her mother's parents into the fight. Both sets of grandparents promised she could live with either of them and they would take good care of her.

Graham simply wasn't willing to take that chance.

Rachel was his responsibility. She was staying in Port Protection and that was final. Having his parents and his former in-laws irritated with him was old news.

But he blamed himself for not paying more attention to what his soon-to-be-punished daughter was doing on the Internet. And he also realized he shouldn't have dismissed Rachel's accusation that he didn't want her to have a life because he didn't have a life of his own.

That was the real reason Courtney Woods sat in the

great room of the lodge now. Rachel obviously assumed if he had a girlfriend from New York City he would give in and move back.

He had news for Rachel.

He would never move back to New York City. And until Rachel reached eighteen and could legally do as she pleased, neither would she.

Graham walked out of the kitchen to where he'd left Courtney. Her chair faced the cathedral-style windows that made up the front of the lodge. The view of the cove and the snowcapped mountains in the distance was spectacular. Yet, Graham suspected the view was the last thing on Courtney's mind at the moment.

She had to be disappointed that love was *not* waiting for her in Alaska as Rachel had led her to believe. Instead, all he had to offer Courtney was a promise that Rachel was going to regret the day she decided to play around with other people's lives.

"Thanks," she said when he handed her the cup.

Graham sat on the chair beside her, aware he should say something—anything—to lessen the gravity of such an awkward situation. He just couldn't think of anything to say.

She saved him the trouble. "You have to give Rachel props for masterminding such a perfect plan. The hearing impaired excuse for why we couldn't talk on the phone was brilliant."

"Yeah, Rachel's a real mastermind, all right," Graham grumbled. "We'll see if she can mastermind her way out of being banned from the Internet for the rest of her life."

She laughed and said, "Well, she definitely used the Internet to her advantage. Your Web site for the lodge, for instance. Rachel backed up her hearing loss story by pointing out your phone number isn't listed on your site."

Graham shook his head in amazement. "The phone number isn't listed any longer because I spent the first six months after I launched the Web site answering calls from people who were only shopping around for rates. I only contact people who are serious enough to e-mail me."

He thought for a minute and said, "Rachel used the Internet to her advantage another way, too. I pay a flat fee for phone and Internet service, so she had no long-distance charges to worry about. And Rachel living with the phone glued to her ear is normal. I had no reason to suspect she wasn't talking to her best friend instead of you."

"Only one thing still bothers me," she said. "Some of the e-mails Rachel sent were..." She paused. "Well, to put it bluntly, they were too mature for a girl her age."

Mature?

Graham gulped.

Did she mean things of a sexual nature?

And how advanced *was* Rachel in that regard? They'd had the *sex talk* when she was twelve. To his relief, the subject had never come up again.

Graham was still trying to summon the courage to ask what she meant by *mature,* when Courtney placed her coffee cup on the end table between their two chairs, bent and picked up her purse from the floor. After pulling out a handful of papers, she unfastened the clip and handed them over.

"Rachel said you could read lips, but I was still worried we would have trouble communicating," she said. "I printed out my favorite e-mails. I wanted to show them to you and tell you how much they touched me. Read them yourself. And then you tell me if those sound like the words of a teenage girl to you."

Graham looked down at the first e-mail.

How would I describe myself?

He winced when familiar words began jumping off the page.

When I look back over my life, I see a man content to let life happen to him, instead of charting his own path. A man who believed by making everyone else happy, he would eventually find happiness himself. But I've come to the realization that life is too precious to leave to chance and life decisions are too important to hand over to someone else. My mistakes have taught me this: choose what you want out of life or life will choose it for you.

"Why, that little thief!" Graham shouted, refusing to bring his now-*red* face up to meet hers. "Rachel took that straight from my journal."

He shifted the papers to the next e-mail:

There are times when such a solitary life leaves me lonelier than I care to admit. Especially on endless, sleepless nights when I gaze at the ceiling, trying to remember how it feels to have the warmth of another body pressed close to mine. Those are the times when I long for a head on my shoulder, another heart beating close to mine, simply enjoying the still of the night.

And the next:

Troubles melt away here in Alaska. Living in such an unspoiled environment renews my spirit, gives me strength, and reminds me of how truly remarkable God's gifts to man really are. The only thing missing is someone to share such an amazing experience.

"Unbelievable," Graham said, shaking his head as he thumbed through the remainder of the pages. He was still too embarrassed to look at her.

Maybe Courtney had been honest enough to admit how embarrassed and how gullible she felt. She'd even explained that if her demanding job had left any time for a personal life, she never would have been curious about the online membership her best friend had given her for her birthday. Still, Graham's embarrassment reached a much deeper level.

A complete stranger had seen right into his soul.

Graham felt as gutted as a fresh fish fillet.

"Let me guess," she said. "Everything I saved came from your journal. Didn't it?"

She'd guessed right.

She reached out and touched his arm, an innocent gesture—unless you hadn't felt a woman's touch in years.

"I don't blame you for being upset about your journal, Graham. Just don't be too hard on Rachel, okay? Be angry with me. I should have paid more attention to other red flags that kept popping up."

Graham finally looked over at her. "What other red flags?"

"Well, mainly the fact that Rachel only e-mailed me

pretending to be you about twice a week. And she covered her bases by telling me how busy you were once fishing season started."

"I am busy once fishing season starts," Graham said. "But I'm still more at fault here than you are. I shouldn't have been too busy to keep up with what my daughter was doing."

"Thanks for trying to make me feel better," she said. "But I insist on paying you for staying at the lodge this weekend. And I'll certainly reimburse you for the plane ticket."

"Absolutely not," Graham said, shaking his head in protest. "If anything, I'm the one who should pay you for your inconvenience in flying all the way across the country. And for your mental anguish over all of this."

"Mental anguish?" she repeated.

He'd obviously said the wrong thing. Her tone had changed from apologetic to terse. And the insulted expression on her face confirmed it.

"Look," she said. "I don't blame you for thinking I'm some desperate love-starved female because Rachel met me through an online dating site. But let's not make this into some big catastrophe that it isn't, okay?"

Graham started to say something, but she didn't give him the chance.

"The way I see it, you and I are the adults here. And I'm pretty sure we'll both survive the weekend without either of us having to go into therapy."

Okay, she'd put him in his place.

Graham began backpedaling as fast as possible. "I don't think you're desperate, or love-starved, or anything else. All I meant by mental anguish was that no one enjoys being the brunt of a joke. I know I don't. Rachel has embarrassed both of us. And I intend to teach her a lesson for being so thoughtless."

She was making him extremely uncomfortable. First, saying how much the words he'd written had touched her. Then, her hand on his arm. Even her plea now to be easy on his daughter.

She was…dammit!

She was being too nice about the whole thing. Plus, she *was* a knockout. She was the type of woman who could knock him right out of his comfortable existence if he gave her half a chance—smart, sexy, bold enough to speak her mind.

But he'd been foolish to think she would spend one second lamenting the fact that Rachel had sent the e-mails instead of him. Career-focused or not, Courtney Woods was *not* the type of woman who had ever been lacking for male attention.

Graham tossed the e-mails onto the table, left his chair and walked to the window a safe distance away from her. It didn't work. She walked up beside him.

They stood in silence, looking out over the cove.

"Rachel isn't as brilliant as you think," Graham said. "I inherited this lodge from my grandfather. He was the one who lost his hearing in one ear from an explosion clearing land for the lodge."

He turned toward her and added, "But tell me the truth about something. Didn't the hearing loss part bother you at all?"

"No," she said. "In fact, I admired you. I found it heroic you hadn't let the accident ruin your life."

Graham let out a long sigh. "Well, at least you didn't

show up because you felt sorry for the poor deaf guy turning forty."

"True," she said. "I only felt sorry for the turning-forty part."

They looked at each other.

And burst out laughing.

It was the icebreaker they'd needed to cut through the tension. And at that moment Graham realized Courtney could have been a real bitch about what Rachel had done. Courtney could have even threatened to sue him. And who would have blamed her? Instead, she was taking it all in stride, far better than he was at the moment.

"This whole thing really is funny when you think about it," she said. "I can't imagine what you were thinking down on the dock when I sounded out every word so carefully, making sure you could read my lips."

Wisely, Graham didn't mention the Russian hooker.

Instead, he said, "I know someone who's going to be reading *my* lips when she gets home. I can promise you that."

"And that's what has me worried," she said.

Graham looked over at her again.

Now she had her arms crossed, tapping the fingers of her right hand impatiently against her left arm. And that's one thing Graham *didn't* miss since he'd dropped out of society—the whole business of trying to figure any woman out.

It was exhausting.

However, if memory served him correctly, her ambiguous statement was his clue to say, "Meaning?"

She looked straight at him and said, "Meaning I'm

not interested in being caught in the middle of a father-daughter fight all weekend, Graham."

"So what are you suggesting? That I just pat Rachel on the head and laugh the whole thing off?"

"I'm suggesting you postpone any punishment until later," she said. "Rachel has really worked hard on your birthday party tomorrow. And I shouldn't tell you this, but she has a special surprise dinner planned for you tonight."

"A dinner?" Graham repeated.

Courtney nodded. "Rachel planned out the menu herself, and I'm supposed to help her cook the meal. I hate to see all of her plans ruined."

"You forget Rachel's *planning* is the reason she's in big trouble right now."

An awkward silence passed between them.

She cocked her head in his direction. "You know, if you really want to teach Rachel a lesson, the best way to do that would be to beat her at her own game."

"I'm not sure what you mean."

"I think we've both figured out the reason I'm here is because Rachel thought if we hit it off, you'd be willing to move back to New York."

"Tell me, Courtney," Graham said. "Is there anything you don't know about me and my daughter?"

She smiled. "I don't know if you're willing to play along with my idea yet."

Okay, one thing he *did* miss since he'd dropped out of society was having a woman smile at him the way Courtney had done now—a flirty little smile, the type of smile only a dead man could resist.

"Keep talking," Graham said.

"What if we let Rachel think her idea worked when

she first gets home? But then we tell her instead of you moving back to New York, I've decided to move to Alaska to be with you?"

Graham laughed. "To quote Rachel's favorite expression, she would totally freak out."

"Exactly." She smiled again.

It took Graham's gaze right back to her moist, pink lips. Memories of that kiss on the dock didn't help Graham's common sense, either. And whether he liked to admit it or not, the knowledge that a beautiful woman like Courtney had flown across the country to meet him was a huge boost to his turning-forty ego.

Why not go along with Courtney's idea?

She was right. It wasn't fair to put her in the middle of their fight all weekend. The situation was already awkward enough.

He'd honor Courtney's request and keep things civil for the weekend. He owed her that much after what Rachel had done. But after Courtney left, Rachel's life was going to change drastically.

And that was a promise.

Graham stuck his hand out. "Okay, it's a deal. Let's show Rachel what it feels like to be on the receiving end of a bad joke."

CHAPTER THREE

THE MINUTE GRAHAM closed the bedroom door after bringing her luggage upstairs, Courtney fished around for her cell phone. She tossed her purse onto the bed and headed for the sliding glass doors that led out to her room's private balcony.

Beth would laugh her ass off at this situation.

But Courtney's mother?

Courtney couldn't even go there.

In fact, coming to Alaska was the first time she'd ever truly crossed her mother, who also happened to be her boss *and* the owner of The Woods Advertising Agency, where Courtney was vice president. Her VP title, however, had nothing to do with being the CEO's daughter. Courtney had earned that title by following faithfully in Lisa Woods's workaholic footsteps.

And she had no life to prove it.

When she couldn't get a signal, Courtney closed her phone and leaned against the railing, thinking back to the night of her birthday party—the real reason behind why she was in Alaska now. They'd celebrated at Courtney's favorite restaurant; Beth, her mother and her mother's constant entourage—the other executives at the agency.

Beth had saved her gift for last. She'd stood to get everyone's attention—as if that were necessary. *Avant-garde* described Beth in every sense of the word; her dark hair in a buzz cut; her jewelry and wardrobe so outrageous she turned heads everywhere she went.

"Courtney likes to claim her being born on Valentine's Day was Cupid's idea of a cruel joke," Beth had said. "She also likes to claim that the reason she's still single is because there aren't any real men left in the world."

Everyone had laughed.

"So I decided to prove her wrong on both accounts," Beth had announced proudly. "Love is out there waiting for her if she'll look for it. And where better to look for real men than the last frontier?"

That's when Beth had held up a printed-out page with Courtney's picture on it—a full-body shot Courtney had forgotten about. Courtney had posed for it when she did an interview for a magazine about the changing trends in advertising—dressed for success and leaning casually back against her desk with a confident smile on her face.

"This," Beth had said, handing Courtney the sheet, "is your new profile page on LoveFromAlaska.com. And when I checked the site an hour ago, you had thirty-five *real* men dying to meet you."

Courtney had thought Beth's gift was hysterical. So had everyone else.

Except, of course, Courtney's mother.

Her mother had remained silent all through dinner. She'd remained silent through the birthday cake dessert. She'd even remained silent during a heated debate about the direction they should take with a new ad campaign when they were having brandy later—and her mother remaining silent during any debate was unprecedented. It wasn't until they were alone in her mother's private town car on the way home from the restaurant, however, that Courtney had received an earful.

"I expect you to cancel the membership to that disgusting dating site immediately before anyone sees it," her mother had demanded. "If word gets out you're peddling yourself on the Internet like some cheap tramp, it would be a total embarrassment to the agency."

"News flash, Mother. Online dating is the norm today." Trying to appease her, Courtney had added, "Besides, it isn't likely any of our clients will be checking out some dating site from Alaska."

"It isn't a risk I'm willing to take," her mother had snipped. "As vice president you have a reputation to uphold and I expect you to do that."

Courtney had assumed the discussion was over.

She hadn't been that lucky.

"What I don't understand," her mother had said, "is where Beth got the idea you wanted some man in your life. If your so-called best friend knew you at all, she'd understand the agency will always be your first priority."

Like mother, like daughter.

The thought had scared the hell out of Courtney.

Within minutes of being dropped off in front of her apartment building, Courtney had her laptop open. And that's when she'd found the first e-mail from Rachel.

Reading what Graham had written about defining what you wanted before life defined it for you had been the equivalent of grabbing Courtney by the shoulders and shaking her until her teeth rattled. In every aspect of her life, in and out of the boardroom, she had the reputation of being assertive and confident—except when it came to her mother. At that exact moment, Courtney knew it was time to cut the cord.

That's why she'd really come to Alaska. She'd come hoping to find herself.

But talk about material for a daytime talk show! She could already hear Dr. Phil now. "And how's online dating working for you so far, Courtney?"

Still, things could have been worse.

Graham could have been a real ass about the whole situation. And who could really blame the poor guy? A crazy e-mail female from New York City had shown up on his dock, not only unannounced, but even demanding to know why he'd lied to her.

Courtney groaned just thinking about it.

At least Graham had agreed to a truce for the weekend. And she would do her best to make sure he didn't regret that decision. She could handle being the peacekeeper, but she didn't want to be the referee.

Especially since, in spite of everything, she was completely smitten with the man she'd come to meet. Graham *had* touched her deeply with his journal entries: his sensitivity; his appreciation of the type of assets you'd never find in some financial portfolio; his insight in being able to look back over his life and identify his mistakes. Plus, now that she'd actually met him, Courtney was so physically attracted to Graham the only way she knew how to describe it was freakishly scary.

And that was so unlike her.

Beth had always accused her of being too picky. Of always finding something not to like about the guys she dated, rather than focusing on things she could learn to like about them.

And maybe she was too picky. She'd just been holding out for that one guy who would make her heart pound, her palms sweat and who completely took her breath away. Courtney had never met such a man.

Until now.

Her thoughts went back to that kiss on the dock. *Her* heart had definitely been pounding. For a second she'd thought Graham was going to kiss her again. She'd seen a little flicker of desire in his eyes signaling there might be some fireworks between them.

Of course, that was before they both knew the whole situation. Now Graham would spend the weekend worried she was some cyber stalker. And she would spend the weekend pretending she wasn't disappointed that he didn't send the e-mails—which, in fact, she was.

But she'd get over it.

The ever-changing world of advertising had taught her one valuable lesson: when things aren't working, take them in a different direction and make them work. Courtney couldn't think of a better time to stick to that principle than now.

She let out a long sigh and remained standing on the balcony, looking out at the shimmering water. She could certainly understand how troubles could melt away here.

Or maybe it was being somewhere so different from New York City. No horns blowing. No streets packed with cars stuck in gridlock traffic. No sidewalks filled with anxious-looking people all scurrying about, cell phones to their ears, hurrying to make that next important meeting or make it to and from work on time.

The only things moving below the lodge were several boats tied to the dock, all bobbing in the water like corks tied to a fishing line. Rachel called the boats skiffs, and Courtney knew Graham used them for his fishing expeditions and for local travel to other communities around Port Protection, since this part of Prince of Wales Island had no road access whatsoever.

She'd been intrigued by the quaint community from the moment she visited the lodge's Web site: the elaborate boardwalk system running throughout the rain forest; the steps called The Stairway to Heaven leading from the boardwalk up to the ridgeline; the pictures of the scenic view from the ridge so beautiful they took your breath away.

Courtney had even imagined climbing that stairway with Graham. She'd fantasized about Graham taking her into his arms and…

Stop it!

No point in going there now.

But Port Protection had captivated her. Almost as much as the picture of Graham that Rachel had chosen for his profile—him standing in the front of the lodge, the look on his face somber, a hint of loneliness in his eyes he couldn't quite hide from the camera.

When Courtney thought about it, loneliness was one of the main reasons she'd kept up the correspondence with Rachel. Her mother had given her the deep-freeze treatment after she'd refused to cancel the membership. But instead of that making Courtney want to reconsider, being estranged from her mother only reinforced how much of Courtney's time her mother truly demanded.

Then Beth had temporarily deserted her.

Beth just had to pick the exact same time to fall madly in lust with a stand-up comic in Atlantic City where Beth ran off to every weekend. Without Beth or her mother demanding her time, Courtney had felt at loose ends.

Had it not been for Rachel, she probably would have caved and begged her mother's forgiveness before they reached some common ground. In a sense, Rachel had saved her from making a grave mistake.

The truth was, Courtney had thoroughly enjoyed being Rachel's mentor of sorts. She had no siblings, no nieces or nephews. Playing the role of a big sister or an aunt to Rachel had been a fun and new experience for her.

And that's why Courtney hoped if she and Graham played a joke on Rachel, they could all laugh about it, call it even and salvage the weekend. Regardless of what Rachel had done, Courtney couldn't wait to finally meet her.

With that thought in mind, Courtney walked into the bedroom where Graham had placed her suitcases on the foot of the bed. Rachel would be home from school within the hour. If Courtney was going to play the role of the happy new girlfriend, she needed to look the part.

But as she headed into the bathroom with her makeup bag to freshen up, Courtney couldn't keep from thinking that being Graham's pretend girlfriend was *not* the role she'd envisioned when she set out for Alaska. Even more disturbing was another thought.

Graham Morrison wouldn't be an easy man to forget.

GRAHAM PLACED A TRAY of appetizers on the dining table in the main room of the lodge—cheese, crackers, some dried dates and figs. He would have done the same for any other guests, making sure something was available to sustain them until time for dinner.

Except Courtney wasn't any other guest.

She was a vibrant, beautiful woman who had him hurrying to his bathroom after she went upstairs, making sure his hygiene wasn't lacking. What shocked Graham was the fact that he'd felt the need to do that.

He'd been so convinced he had everything he needed living in Port Protection. That a woman was the last thing he wanted in his life. Yet, all Courtney had to do was smile at him a couple of times and he was scurrying off to shave and brush his teeth and change his shirt.

But then, Graham reasoned, maybe if he had female guests at the lodge on a regular basis, he would have automatically done the same thing. He'd never been a slob, but shaving in the middle of the day for a bunch of smelly fishermen was plain laughable.

What wasn't laughable was the knowledge Courtney had flown all the way from New York to meet him. Talk about putting pressure on a guy.

Plus, who knew what Rachel had been telling Courtney about him for the past three months—other than the fact he was deaf, and Courtney had claimed she found that heroic. It only made sense he would be a little self-conscious, maybe even a little intimidated.

Courtney had come expecting to meet a hero who had overcome all the obstacles in his life. She'd found instead a clueless father who wasn't even savvy enough to realize what his teenage daughter was doing on the Internet.

In fact, the woman upstairs was basically a complete stranger, yet she knew more things about him than most people ever would. Private things. Things he never would have shared with anyone else. And he knew virtually nothing about her.

Except she was an advertising executive from New York.

And he liked the way she kissed.

But he wasn't going to revisit the damn kiss again. She'd caught him off guard, that's all. And brushing his teeth didn't mean he hoped she would kiss him again.

After Courtney found out what a disaster she'd walked into, she'd made it clear all she wanted to do for the rest of the weekend was fly under the radar until she could head back to New York City on Monday. And Graham intended to do his best to see she did just that.

He'd be a gracious host. He'd be a charming conversationalist at dinner. He'd even be the life of his own damn birthday party if that's what it took to get them through the weekend.

But after Courtney left, he was going to *kill* his daughter. Not literally, of course. He was only going to make Rachel wish she were dead.

No TV. No Internet. No iPod. No phone.

No *anything* fun or entertaining.

Not until Graham was fully satisfied that Rachel was truly sorry for the stupid stunt she'd pulled. Whether Rachel liked it or not, he was still her father. And whether Rachel liked it or not, until she turned eighteen, he made all the rules.

CHAPTER FOUR

RACHEL JUMPED OUT OF her seat the second the bell rang. She didn't wait to walk home with her good friend Tiki Iya the way she usually did.

Today, Rachel left her classroom and hurried outside to the wide boardwalk meandering through Port Protection like a railroad track. She smiled when she found her absolute *best* friend waiting for her in his usual spot.

The Alaskan husky wagged his tail as Rachel approached. Rachel bent down and rubbed the big dog's ears affectionately when she walked up beside him.

Her father had surprised her with her own puppy shortly after they'd arrived in Port Protection. It was his way of proving there were things she could have in Alaska that she couldn't have back home. She'd named the pup Broadway—her message to her father that no matter where he made her live, her heart would *always* belong to New York City.

That had been five years ago.

Rachel was still as homesick as the day she left.

"Let's go, boy," Rachel told the dog.

With Broadway in the lead she headed for the lodge, a prayer on her lips that this would be the last year she spent in a school with only twenty-one students. Even worse was being the *only* high school sophomore.

That meant she would also be the only high school junior next year. And unless someone her own age moved to Port Protection—about as likely as her dad agreeing to let her have her nose pierced—her graduating class would consist of a big whopping *one!*

Available boys?

Forgetaboutit!

Boys her age in Port Protection were nonexistent. Just like her totally nonexistent social life.

"Rachel. Wait up."

Rachel turned to find Tiki running toward her. Her friend had the black hair and eyes and coloring of her Haida ancestors. Tiki's Haida name was *dukdukdiya,* which meant *hummingbird,* because she was so little. Although Tiki was two years younger, the age difference hadn't kept them from becoming close friends. In fact, if it hadn't been for Tiki, Rachel knew she never would have survived living in Port Protection.

She was, however, beginning to regret confiding in Tiki about her plan to get her father to move back to New York. Tiki had warned her from the beginning the online dating idea was crazy.

And Tiki did so *love* being right.

Taking a second to recover from her race to catch up, Tiki said between breaths, "Why are you in such a big hurry to get home, silly? You know your dad is going to kill you."

Rachel rolled her eyes.

"I'd be terrified," Tiki said, pretending a shudder. "I

can't even imagine what my dad would do if I charged a plane ticket on his credit card."

"Oh, please," Rachel said. "The charge on Dad's credit card is the least of it. What will totally freak him out is me pretending to be him and inviting Courtney to his birthday party."

"But aren't you worried Courtney is going to be mad at you, too? You lied to her from the beginning."

"I know," Rachel admitted. "But Courtney really likes me. We've spent hours talking on the phone. And when I explain I was only trying to get Dad to move back to civilization, I think she'll forgive me."

"For your sake, I hope you're right."

"Of course, I'm right," Rachel said, trying to convince herself more than Tiki. "Courtney isn't some phony, shallow person or she would have lost interest the second I told her Dad had lost his hearing. She doesn't even mind Dad having a teenage daughter. I'm telling you, Tiki, the woman is a saint."

"Let's just hope your dad thinks so."

"Yeah, I can always hope," Rachel said with a snort. "But if I know Dad, all he's going to do is be mad at me and sulk. And then he'll spend the whole weekend stomping around like an old bull, ignoring me *and* Courtney completely."

Tiki looked over at her. "And that's what I've never understood about this plan of yours, Rachel. If you didn't think your dad was going to like Courtney, why even bother?"

"Because I'm desperate, Tiki. And if I push a gorgeous woman like Courtney in front of Dad, maybe he'll remember what it's like to have a real life."

"And if he doesn't?"

Rachel sighed. "Then at least I've shown Dad what it feels like to have someone else make decisions for him without his consent."

"But what if your dad started stomping around like an old bull when Courtney got here and she got back on the plane and left?"

Rachel scoffed. "Do you really think I'm that stupid? I've been planning this day for months. I made Gil promise that under no circumstances would he let Courtney get back on that plane."

They stopped walking when they reached the fork where the boardwalk divided. Broadway obediently sat to wait. A left turn led to Trail's End Lodge. A right turn led to one of the more populated sections of Port Protection where Tiki lived.

Rachel shifted her book bag to her shoulder. "Well, at least wish me luck."

"Luck?" Tiki laughed. "Forget luck, Rachel. What you need is a freaking miracle."

Still laughing, Tiki headed off down the boardwalk.

"So *not* funny," Rachel called after her.

But as Rachel headed home, the situation was becoming less funny with every step she took. Sure, she knew her dad was going to be furious with her—that was a given. She was just counting on her dad's good manners not to make a scene with Courtney there.

Only now Tiki had put other doubts in her mind.

What if Courtney didn't forgive her for lying? What if instead of being a saint, Courtney turned out to be some screaming psycho chick and really did flip out over what she'd done?

Rachel didn't have to pretend a shudder.

She slowed her pace, wondering if maybe Tiki was right. Maybe she shouldn't be in such a big hurry to get to the lodge. Maybe she should be late on purpose and give both her dad and Courtney more time to calm down.

Yes.

Maybe she should let her dad and Courtney think she was too afraid to show up. That should gain a little sympathy—hopefully, from both of them. And if her dad and Courtney were worried about her, maybe they'd be less likely to be so angry.

Pleased with her new plan, Rachel looked down at Broadway. "Want to go on a long walk, boy?"

The big dog barked and wagged his tail.

COURTNEY NIBBLED FROM the appetizer tray she'd found waiting for her when she'd come downstairs. Graham had arranged everything perfectly—even had a glass of white wine waiting for her. It had been the exact pick-me-up she needed after her long trip.

She'd been impressed by the gesture, even if catering to his guests was part of Graham's everyday life. But who was she kidding?

Everything about Graham Morrison impressed her.

She glanced in his direction again as she finished off her last bite of cheese, and she couldn't help but smile inwardly over the fact that he'd changed his shirt and shaved while she'd been upstairs. Her only regret was that he'd hardly said a word to her. Instead, he'd been pacing back and forth at the lodge's front window for the past thirty minutes.

He looked at his watch for the fiftieth time, frowned

and finally looked in her direction. "I'm getting worried," he said. "Rachel should have been home by now."

Courtney didn't want to pooh-pooh Graham's concern, but common sense told her Rachel was dragging her feet coming home on purpose. That's what she would have done had she been in Rachel's teenage shoes.

"I'm sure Rachel's okay, Graham. Broadway wouldn't let anything happen to her."

She'd been trying to assure him Rachel was safe, but now he was frowning again.

And this time he was frowning at *her*.

"You just mentioned Broadway," he said. "I was joking earlier, but Rachel really has told you everything about our lives here, hasn't she?"

Courtney didn't blame him for being upset that she knew so much about him—even the name of his dog. In his situation, she would have felt violated, too. Particularly over his journal entries. She wouldn't bring up the e-mails again.

But maybe if she gave Graham the opportunity to ask a few questions about her, he might not feel so exposed. Deciding to give him that opportunity, Courtney left her chair and walked over to where Graham stood.

"I can understand how unsettling it must be for me to know so much about you when you know nothing about me," she said.

Was it her imagination, or was he staring at her lips?

"So?" Courtney offered. "Is there anything you do want to ask about me, Graham?"

"Yes," he said. "Why would a successful career woman from New York want to get involved with some deaf guy from Alaska and his bratty teenage daughter?"

Courtney laughed. "Well, when you put it that way, it makes me wonder why myself." She paused before she added, "You have an amazing daughter, Graham, even though you're upset with her right now. In fact, for the past three months, Rachel has been the one bright spot in my day."

His expression softened slightly. "Even when she was complaining about her horrible life here?" he asked.

Is that what was bothering him? Was Graham worried Rachel had aired all of their dirty laundry? If that was the problem, she could clear that misconception up real quick.

"You have my word, Graham," Courtney said, "never once has Rachel said anything but wonderful things about you."

He didn't look convinced. "Only because she was trying to sell you on me."

"Believe me," Courtney said, "it wasn't a hard sale."

The words just hung there.

Courtney couldn't take them back.

And Graham didn't seem to know what to say.

Thankfully a loud bark defused the situation.

"Showtime," Courtney said, moving closer to Graham and sliding her arm around his waist.

"And how far are we going to take this?" he asked.

"Far enough to be convincing until you tell her the truth."

Graham put his arm around her shoulder. And his arm did feel good around her—too good. Courtney breathed in his scent—all manly and intoxicating. And though she knew she was only torturing herself, Courtney couldn't help but notice how perfectly they fit together.

"Now what?" he asked, snapping her back to reality.

"Smile and look happy," Courtney said.

BROADWAY BOUNDED THROUGH the front door first and ran straight to her father. Rachel stopped dead in her tracks. She simply couldn't believe what she was seeing.

Her dad?

Smiling from ear to ear?

In a clutch with a woman he'd just met?

Unfreakingbelievable!

All Rachel could do was stare.

"Well, aren't you going to say hello to Courtney?" her dad asked as if she weren't late getting home.

"Hi," Rachel managed, but it came out as a squeak.

"Come here, you," Courtney said.

Before Rachel knew what was happening, Courtney flew across the room and engulfed her in a big hug. And when she let Rachel go, she stepped back and smiled.

"I'm so happy to finally meet you, Rachel," she gushed. "You're even prettier in person than you are in your pictures."

"Thanks," was all Rachel could think to say.

Although Rachel doubted Courtney really cared. Miss So-Happy-To-Meet-You had already hurried back across the room to wrap herself around dear old Dad again.

"We have every right to be angry with you, young lady," her father said.

Rachel held her breath, expecting the worst.

What she got instead was another big smile.

"But how can we be angry," he added, "when you're the one responsible for bringing us together?"

"It was love at first sight," Courtney said.

"Totally," her dad agreed.

Huh?

Rachel couldn't believe it. Not only was her dad still grinning like some silly buffoon, but he had just said *totally* for the first time in his life. Had he completely lost his mind? That was the only explanation Rachel had for his goofy behavior.

"In fact," he said, "Courtney and I have already decided now that we've found each other, we don't want to be apart for a minute. Right, Courtney?"

"Absolutely," Courtney said, smiling up at him.

And then he kissed her.

On the mouth!

In a flash, Rachel was mentally packing her bags. She could see herself running through Central Park with Broadway. And she *would* take Broadway back to New York with her. Millions of people had dogs in the city no matter what her dad said.

Other images quickly filled her head.

She could order Chinese takeout any hour of the day or night—and man, how she had missed Chinese takeout. She could shop on Fifth Avenue. She could go to the Met anytime she wanted. She could see a musical on the real Broadway. And attend the Christmas tree lighting at Rockefeller Center for the first time in years. She could even be in Times Square for the big ball drop on New Year's Eve.

Rachel was on the verge of jumping up and down. She couldn't wait to tell Tiki. She really had been granted a freaking miracle. Finally, she could go to a regular high school with boys and girls her own age. Finally, she could experience what it was like to be a *normal* teenager.

"Courtney's agreed to move to Alaska to be with us. Isn't that great?"

"What?" Rachel shrieked.

And that's when she saw her dad's expression change before her eyes. Now his jaw was rigid—his smile gone. And the reaction Rachel had been expecting all along quickly followed.

"A lie isn't so funny when you're on the receiving end of that lie, is it, Rachel?"

Rachel balled her fists together. He was using his serious father-knows-best voice. She *hated* when he did that.

"And save yourself the trouble of thinking up any more schemes," he warned. "We are *not* moving back to New York under any circumstances. And that's final."

For one brief second, Rachel truly hated her father.

"You can't control my life forever!" Rachel screamed back at him. "When I turn eighteen I *will* move to New York City. And I'll never come back to this miserable place again. Ever. *That's* final!"

Sobbing, Rachel ran from the room.

Faithfully, Broadway trotted after her.

CHAPTER FIVE

COURTNEY FLINCHED WHEN a door slammed in the distance. Slowly, she and Graham untangled themselves, then quickly stepped away from each other.

"That went well, didn't it?" was all he said.

He didn't mention that second kiss.

Neither did Courtney. She'd analyze the kiss later. At the moment, her only concern was Rachel.

"I had no idea Rachel would be so upset when I talked you into teasing her, Graham. I need to go apologize."

"*Apologize?* Don't be ridiculous. Rachel's the one who needs to apologize to *you.*"

"And I'm sure Rachel will," Courtney said. "But I'm not very proud of myself right now for making her cry."

He started to object again, but Courtney stopped him.

"Please, let me talk to her. If you don't, it's going to be a miserable weekend for all of us."

Graham kept staring at her.

Courtney held his gaze.

"Go through the kitchen," he finally said, pointing across the great room to the saloon-style doors. "There's a hallway off the kitchen. Rachel's bedroom door is the first door on the right."

"Thank you," Courtney told him sincerely.

"But when you're through talking to her," he said, "tell Rachel I want to see her in my office. No excuses."

Courtney nodded and started toward the kitchen. When she reached the hallway, she could have found Rachel's room without Graham's directions. Broadway was stretched out on the floor, guarding the door.

Courtney bent and gave the big dog's head a fond pat. And only after Broadway wagged his tail in permission did she stand up and place a gentle knock above a sign that read: Teenzilla Inside—Enter at Your Own Risk.

The first knock failed to produce a response.

Courtney knocked again. "Rachel, it's Courtney. Can I come in for a minute?"

"Go away!"

This time Courtney turned the doorknob and Broadway saw his chance. By the time Courtney stepped inside the room, Broadway had already launched himself onto the bed beside his mistress.

Rachel's tearstained face made Courtney wince.

"I owe you an apology, Rachel. It was my idea to play a joke on you, not your father's. It was a mean thing to do and I'm sorry."

"It doesn't matter," Rachel said, swiping at her eyes with the back of her hand. "I played a mean joke on you. I deserved it."

Courtney walked across the room. Without being invited, she sat on the edge of Rachel's bed. "If it makes any difference, I'm still glad I came. I wouldn't have missed meeting you for anything."

Rachel's chin came up. "Really?"

"Really," Courtney said, reaching for her hand.

"After all, you and I have more or less been dating for three months now."

That comment at least got a half smile out of her. Then Rachel's face clouded over again, reminding Courtney how much she looked like her father. Same ink-black hair. Same brown eyes with the same hint of sadness if you looked closely enough.

Rachel sniffed and said, "Dad's really pissed at me, isn't he?"

Courtney nodded. "And I'm afraid I only made things worse. I'm sorry, Rachel. I printed out some of the e-mails you sent me that I thought were from your dad."

Rachel gasped. "And you showed them to him?"

"Sorry."

Rachel flopped back against her pillow with a loud groan. "Now he really is going to kill me. I took stuff from his journal."

"I know. Graham told me," Courtney said. "And I hope you realize how wrong that was. Everyone deserves the right to privacy."

Rachel sat up. "And what about my rights? Every day Dad keeps me here he's violating my right to life, liberty and the pursuit of happiness."

Courtney smiled knowingly. "How'd you do on your American history test, by the way?"

"Aced it, of course," Rachel said, but her tone was still surly.

"Do you really hate living here so much?"

"Wouldn't you?"

Courtney shrugged. "Actually, I think living here might be a nice change from the city."

Rachel snorted. "Yeah, but we're not talking about

a nice change. Dad would keep me here permanently if he could."

"Only because he loves you, Rachel. And he wants to keep you safe."

"I'm sick and tired of being safe!"

But neither of them mentioned what had led up to Graham moving them to Alaska. It was easier to talk about things like that on the phone than it was in person. The phone provided the barrier a person needed to keep anyone else from seeing their pain.

In one of their more serious conversations, Rachel had told Courtney that her mother had been shot and killed in a robbery outside their apartment building when Rachel was only ten. She'd said Graham had quit his brokerage firm on Wall Street, put their apartment on Park Avenue up for sale and had moved them to Alaska immediately after the funeral, despite strong objections from Graham's parents and his in-laws.

In fact, now that Courtney thought about it, not once had losing his wife been mentioned in any of the e-mails that were supposedly from Graham—another red flag that should have warned her something wasn't right. Instead, Courtney had assumed talking about the tragedy was still too painful for him.

But now Courtney understood.

Rachel hadn't tried to express her father's feelings because she had no idea how her father felt about her mother's death. Graham obviously hadn't shared those feelings with his daughter.

"You don't really agree that Dad should keep me here all through high school, do you?"

The question pulled Courtney back from her thoughts.

"Something could happen to me right here in Port Protection, you know. I could get eaten by a bear. Or attacked by a wolf. Or I could drown if a whale turned the skiff over and spend eternity in a watery grave at the bottom of the ocean. I could even have my eyes pecked out by a hungry eagle."

Rachel sighed a dramatic sigh.

"Or," she said with a pitiful look on her face, "I can continue to die a slow and painful death the way I'm doing now."

Courtney had to laugh. "You certainly know how to paint a grim picture."

"Living here is a grim picture," Rachel mumbled.

"Then let's change that. At least for this weekend. I came for a party. And I'm not going to let you or your dad cheat me out of that. You've told me so much about all of the colorful characters in Port Protection, I'm really going to be upset if I've come all this way and I never get to meet them."

Finally, Rachel smiled.

"Like Snag Horton with his big gold front tooth?"

"Yes," Courtney said. "I want to meet Snag."

"And what about Fat Man Jack?"

Courtney laughed. "Were you teasing me? Or did he really have to have a special boat built to hold him?"

"Wouldn't you if you weighed six hundred pounds?"

"I'd love to meet Fat Man Jack," Courtney said. "And your friend Tiki."

"You're really going to love Tiki's parents," Rachel said. "Tiki's dad has been my dad's best friend since they were kids when dad spent all his summers here. Yanoo doesn't say much, but you'll like him. And Tiki's mom is way cool like you. Hanya really gets Tiki just like you understand me."

"And your adopted grandparents are still okay with you having your dad's party at their general store?"

Rachel nodded. "I told Peg and Hal we'd come early tomorrow and put up all the decorations."

"We aren't going to have a party or your surprise dinner tonight unless you go make peace with your dad. He wants to see you in his office as soon as we finish talking."

"Great," Rachel grumbled. "I can't wait."

"You owe your dad a huge apology, Rachel," Courtney said. "And you know it."

A deep sigh escaped Rachel's lips.

"And he could have been nasty to me, but he wasn't."

Rachel rolled her eyes.

"And if I didn't adore you, I could have been nasty about this whole situation, too," Courtney reminded her. "Do you realize how embarrassed I was when your dad had no idea I even existed?"

"Okay, okay." Rachel groaned. "I'll go make peace with Dad. But *only* because I owe it to you."

Courtney reached out and gave Rachel a big hug.

To Courtney's relief, Rachel hugged her back.

"Could you do me one more favor?"

Rachel nodded.

"Do you still have any of the e-mails on file that I thought I was sending to your dad?"

Rachel got up from the bed and walked over to her dresser. Seconds later, she pulled out a folder from her bottom dresser drawer. "I was afraid Dad might catch me, so I always printed them out before I erased them and waited to read them later."

"Devious of you," Courtney said, "but perfect for what I have in mind. Would you give them to your dad for me?"

Rachel looked concerned. "But why?"

"Because I wrote those e-mails thinking I was writing them to your dad. And Graham has the right to see them."

Rachel grinned. "Tell me the truth. Are you crushin' on my dad, Courtney?"

"I'm just trying to even the score a little. I know a lot about Graham. It's only fair he should have a chance to know who I am. If he wants to know anything about me, of course," Courtney added quickly.

"Adults are so weird," Rachel said. "But whatever."

"And one more thing," Courtney said. "I know you want to dress up for dinner tonight, but I really wouldn't push your dad about that. I think he's had enough of both of us for one day. Let's just concentrate on making him the really nice dinner you've planned."

Rachel shook her head. "No way. We *are* dressing up for dinner. And Dad will just have to get over it."

GRAHAM LEANED BACK in his chair, his feet propped up on his desk. He'd been waiting for Rachel for—he checked his watch—thirty-five minutes now. If she didn't show up soon, he'd walk down the hall and get her himself.

He still wasn't sure how he felt about Courtney's obvious affection for his daughter. She'd defended Rachel at every turn. And though Graham admired Courtney for doing that, it puzzled him.

What was the common bond there?

She skirted around the question when he'd asked earlier, saying only that Rachel had been a bright spot in her day. Not that he questioned her honesty. She'd already proven she was blunt enough to tell him how she felt.

Like telling him he wasn't a hard sale. Graham smiled, thinking about it.

Until he looked down at his watch again. Five o'clock already. If Rachel didn't get her butt in gear soon, they were going to be having her big surprise birthday dinner for breakfast.

Rachel's planning dinner was another mystery to Graham. His daughter had never shown any interest in the kitchen. Not even when her mother was alive.

A wave of guilt suddenly washed over him. He wasn't being fair, and Graham knew it. Rachel never had the opportunity to have any time in the kitchen with her mother and Julia hadn't been the in-the-kitchen type.

In fact, both of their careers had been so demanding they'd always had a live-in housekeeper even when they were first married—him the new face on Wall Street, Julia the brilliant new prosecuting attorney determined to make a name for herself. And later, after Rachel was born, a daytime nanny had been added to the staff to care for the child who didn't quite fit in with a busy and successful couple's schedules.

And that's what Graham didn't understand about Rachel's damn insistence to return to New York. Why would Rachel want to go back to a life like that? A life so busy you had no time for family? Seeing each other only in passing? Losing sight of yourself and the people most important to you?

Well, not him—not ever.

What had appeared to be the good life on the surface had been far from perfect, regardless of the happy childhood memories Rachel had about living across the street from Central Park. He'd never tarnish those memories. Just as he'd never tell Rachel that her parents' marriage had been on shaky ground from the very beginning.

As with the rest of his past life, he and Julia had sort of happened to each other. They'd both moved in the same social circle, and their parents had been good friends. Marriage had seemed like the next logical step, and they'd taken it. But their marriage had always been based more on what everyone else expected of them than on any true love for each other.

Sadly, it had taken Julia's death before Graham realized what a meaningless life he had fallen into. He'd had his priorities completely out of order. He'd placed his career and the almighty dollar above his ten-year-old daughter, whose care had been the responsibility of a long string of housekeepers and nannies instead of her own parents.

He'd failed at marriage.

He would *not* fail as a father.

He'd left New York and never looked back. And he'd come to the one place where he'd always felt centered even as a kid, thanks to his grandfather Morrison. His grandfather had been an unpretentious man who firmly believed that nature and the simple things in life fed a person's soul and shaped their true character.

Graham had wanted Rachel to experience those same values. And he knew Rachel had been happy the first couple of years, when having her father's full attention had been a novelty instead of a curse. Graham also knew most of Rachel's attitude about being stuck in Port Protection now was simply her being a teenager.

Still, the thought of Rachel returning to New York turned Graham inside out.

He wanted to keep her safe.

And not only from the type of crime everyone faced living in a large city. Graham wanted to keep Rachel safe from getting caught up in the whole gotta-have-it-all-regardless-of-the-cost madness that skewed a person's outlook on life.

He'd lived that type of phony existence.

He'd also been raised by a long string of housekeepers and nannies, and he'd been born to parents who still believed money, power and social standing were the measure of a person's worth. In turn, he'd married a woman who met his parents' approval and who shared those same beliefs.

Had he stayed in New York, Graham knew he wouldn't have stood a chance against interference from his parents and from his former in-laws. Had he stayed, it would have been too tempting to fall back into his old routine instead of taking full responsibility for his daughter.

Before Rachel set out on her journey through life, Graham wanted to do for her what his grandfather had done for him. He wanted to teach his daughter that there was so much more to life than an impressive salary, or a luxury penthouse apartment, or a closet filled with designer clothes. He wanted Rachel to know who she was as a person. And the longer he kept Rachel in Alaska, Graham believed, the better chance she would have of learning to appreciate the things that no amount of money, power or social standing could buy.

A loud knock brought Graham upright in his chair.

Speak of the devil.

He prepared himself for another shouting match.

Instead, the first thing Rachel said when she closed his office door was, "I'm so sorry, Dad. For everything. Especially for copying text from your journal."

"Sorry is a good place to start."

Her chin came up in defiance. "Well, at least Courtney has forgiven me."

"Courtney's a nicer person than I am."

Rachel mumbled something under her breath.

Graham let it go. "What were you thinking, Rachel? Did you really expect me to take one look at Courtney and fall in love with her?"

"Well, I…uh—" She looked down at the folder she was rolling and unrolling nervously in her hands. When she looked back up she said, "Okay, yes. I did think you would fall in love with Courtney. How could you not fall for her, Dad? She's smart. She's pretty. She's funny. She's perfect for you. Just like Meg Ryan was perfect for Tom Hanks in *You've Got Mail.*"

At least one mystery had been solved—where Rachel had come up with her insane e-mail idea.

"But real life isn't a movie, Rachel," he lectured. "In real life people pick their own partners. And if I ever decide to fall in love with someone, *I'll* decide who's perfect for me."

She tossed her hair and said, "In other words, you don't like someone else making decisions for you, right?"

"Right."

"Neither do I, Dad."

He'd walked right into that one. But Graham wasn't about to let Rachel take control of the conversation.

"The difference," Graham pointed out, "is that I'm

the father, you're the child, and it's my duty to make decisions for you until you're old enough to make them for yourself."

"No, Dad," she said. "I was a child when we first moved here. But I'm not a child anymore. And that's the problem. As long as I stay here, my life isn't going anywhere. And you don't seem to care."

Graham swallowed the big lump in his throat. Is that what Rachel really thought? That he didn't care how she felt?

"You're wrong," Graham said. "I do care. You're the most important thing in my life, Rachel, and I love you. And because I do love you, there are going to be times when I have to do what I think is best. Can't you understand that?"

"No," she said, crossing her arms stubbornly. "But obviously there isn't anything I can do about it."

"I'm glad you've figured that out," Graham said, his voice stern now. "Because what you did to Courtney is inexcusable. I hope you're ashamed of yourself."

Her head dropped as she looked down at the floor. "I said I was sorry."

"Sorry isn't good enough," Graham said. "But you have Courtney to thank for me postponing any punishment until after the weekend. You invited her, and I expect you to bend over backward to make sure she has a good time while she's here."

She looked up again, her expression more repentant this time. "I will, Dad, I promise. And thanks for being so nice to Courtney in spite of being mad at me. She really has been a good friend to me."

"That's what has me concerned," Graham admitted.

"I don't need another woman agreeing with you that you should move to New York. Both of your grandmothers do enough of that already. It only makes you more unhappy living here."

"But Courtney isn't like MiMi and Gram at all, Dad. Courtney tells me all the time I should stop worrying about New York and focus on making life in Port Protection work for me while I'm here."

"Excellent advice," Graham said a little too quickly.

"Shocker." Rachel snorted. "Of course *you* would think Courtney's advice is excellent."

Graham grinned in spite of himself.

Rachel only rolled her eyes.

But they both knew this storm had passed—at least for now. And like all parents and children who instinctively know when it's time to move on from an argument, Graham stood and held his arms out. Rachel stepped around his desk and walked into them.

"Don't ever think that I don't care about your feelings," Graham said, pulling his daughter close as he kissed the top of her head. "But for now you and I are going to have to agree to disagree on you staying in Alaska. Is that a deal?"

"Maybe," Rachel said, pushing away from him. "I'll agree to disagree, if you'll agree to something." She stuck her hand out. "Deal?"

Graham looked at her outstretched hand, then back at Rachel. "Agree to what?"

"I'm making you a special birthday dinner tonight," she said proudly. "And I want to dress up as if we were going out to some fancy restaurant in New York. If I can't go to New York, I'll bring New York here to Port Protection."

Graham shrugged. "Okay. Dress anyway you want."

He reached out to shake on the deal. Rachel jerked her hand back.

"I meant I want *you* to dress for dinner, too, Dad. That's the deal. And don't say you don't have anything nice to wear."

"I don't have anything to wear."

"Yes, you do. You have a tuxedo in your closet."

"And what were you doing in my closet?"

Rachel grimaced. "Sorry. But I saw the tux when I was looking for your journal."

She ran for the door after that confession, but she stopped, hurried back and placed the folder she'd been mutilating on his desk. "I almost forgot. Courtney wanted me to give you those. They're the e-mails she wrote when she thought she was writing them to you."

Graham was still staring at the folder when Rachel reached the door. He didn't look up until she said his name.

"Dinner will be ready at seven." She flashed him a big grin. "That gives you plenty of time to clean up and put on your tux."

"I am not wearing a tux!" Graham called out as the door closed behind her.

What the hell?

Graham shook his head. His day kept getting crazier by the minute.

First, Courtney had kissed him senseless the second she stepped off the plane. Then, he'd learned his own flesh and blood had put him up for auction on the Internet. Next, he'd been informed Rachel had suddenly decided to become Martha Stewart. And now he'd been told he had to wear a tux to dinner.

Rachel had brought New York to Port Protection, all right. Up close and personal! Glancing at the folder again only made Graham wonder why Courtney wanted him to read the e-mails. Was she trying to give him a better idea of who she was? Or had that second kiss sent her the wrong message that he was interested?

Graham sat behind his desk.

And why had he kissed Courtney that second time? He hadn't *meant* to kiss her. He'd just been standing there, his arm around her, and she'd been smiling at him. And dammit, he just couldn't help himself.

Is that what turning forty did to a man?

Did hitting the big four-oh unleash some hidden gene that suddenly made a man feel the need to prove his virility? Or had he only been fooling himself all along? Had he really come to Alaska for Rachel's protection? Or had he been protecting himself by making sure he wouldn't have the opportunity to feel anything for a woman again?

He needed a clear head. He had to stop overanalyzing every little thing—worrying about his reaction to this and his reaction to that. Of course, he was attracted to Courtney.

He had eyes, didn't he?

His reaction was no different than any other healthy man's reaction to a good-looking woman. He'd been out of circulation so long he'd forgotten what was normal and what wasn't.

And that sent Graham's gaze back to the folder again.

Okay. He'd read Courtney's e-mails. It wasn't as

though he had anything pressing to do at the moment, since Rachel and Courtney were fixing dinner. He had another hour to kill before he had to *dress* for dinner.

And yes, he would wear the tux.

Begrudgingly, but he'd wear it. He'd never tell Rachel, but he would wear a tux to dinner every night until she left for college if that's what it took to improve her bad attitude.

Graham picked up the folder before he changed his mind. And leaning back in his chair, he propped his feet up on his desk again and opened to Courtney's first e-mail.

Hi Graham.
The way I would describe myself is being in total awe over everything you said about life in your introductory e-mail to me. You see, today happens to be my thirty-fifth birthday. And if anyone needs to get her whole life-act together, it's moi.
I'm also one of those people who assumed by making everyone else happy, I'd eventually find happiness myself. Your e-mail has snapped me out of that delusion.
So, thank you, Graham.
You appear to be a wise and thoughtful man.
I hope we can become good friends.

The next one read:

You mentioned those nights when you stare at the ceiling, unable to sleep. Sleep has never come easy for me. Sometimes I'm lonely. Sometimes I'm just plain terrified at how quickly life is passing me by. I blink and my day is gone. Two blinks and another year has passed. I have this recurring dream where I'm sitting on a white cloud. I know I'm dead, but when I open my book of life all of the pages are blank. They say bad dreams are only mental snapshots of your worst fears, and I believe that. If I had the courage to be honest with myself, my worst fear is that my blank pages will never be filled.

Courtney had said his words touched her.

Ditto.

He often felt as if his life had been a blank page until he moved to Alaska. Was it possible Courtney's trip to Alaska represented the same for her? Had she hoped to start a new chapter in her life and fill some of those pages?

Graham could only wonder.

But thinking about Courtney reminded him he would soon be facing her again at dinner. And deciding he'd better see if he could still fit into his damn tux after five years, Graham got up from his chair and headed for his bedroom.

He took the folder with him. If he couldn't sleep tonight, Courtney's e-mails would keep him company.

CHAPTER SIX

RACHEL HAD PAID CLOSE attention to their reactions when her dad and Courtney saw each other for the first time all dressed up for dinner—her dad handsome in his tux; Courtney fab in a totally to-die-for off-the-shoulder black dress, her hair in a knot on top of her head. It was like watching a scene straight out of *Pretty Woman*—the one where Richard Gere sees Julia Roberts in that fancy red cocktail dress for the first time and she's all smiling at him because he's so wickedly hot she just can't stand it. Rachel loved those old romance movies from before she was born, but she especially loved that one.

Rachel was wearing a fancy red dress tonight, too—not as fancy as the one Julia wore in the movie—a dress her MiMi had sent her with a note that said:

> Even if you have no use for a fancy dress in dreadful Port Protection, darling, it's your favorite color and I thought of you the second I saw it.

Her dad had freaked over the note, saying with friends like MiMi he didn't need any enemies. But her dad had never really gotten along with her mom's mom anyway.

Now they had just finished dinner and dessert and she

could tell her dad had really enjoyed it. He'd even said the menu was worthy of being served at any classy restaurant in New York City, but he didn't realize how true his statement was.

She'd searched the Web sites of fancy New York restaurants for hours putting her menu together. The melt-in-your-mouth roasted salmon with a mustard, tarragon and chive sauce was compliments of a restaurant called L'Appétit. She'd chosen the fish because during salmon season they had the stuff practically coming out of their ears. The vegetable and rice medley—veggie ribbons on ice—had been on the menu of a restaurant named Wellington's, and she'd chosen the dish first because she loved the cute name of it and second, because they had squash and zucchini from the garden and her dad had always preferred rice to potatoes.

Her adopted grandmother Peg had made the apple cobbler for her, and Rachel was glad. Although the meal had been fairly easy to prepare with Courtney's help, they never would have had time to make cobbler.

Yes, her meal had been a great success.

But right now Rachel was disappointed.

She'd also searched the Internet for ways to make a table setting intimate—God, but she loved the word *intimate.* She'd kept the overhead lighting off, and to "set the mood" she'd placed candles on half of their long dining table so her dad and Courtney would be forced to sit at one end. Her dad was in his usual place at the head, and Courtney was sitting right beside him—so close they could have held hands, which was looking more doubtful with every minute.

The *mood* she'd created wasn't working.

Sure, her dad and Courtney had been talking to each other all through dinner about different places they'd been in Europe, about books they'd read recently, and other boring adult blah, blah, blah. But at this rate, if Rachel didn't do something quick, all of her romantic candlelight was going to be wasted.

She had to get their focus back on each other—the way it had been when Courtney had first come downstairs for dinner. When her dad picked up his wineglass again and Courtney dabbed at the corner of her mouth with her napkin, Rachel saw her chance.

"So?" Rachel said. "Do you think there's a possibility you guys might hook up after all?"

Courtney laughed.

Her dad choked on his wine and sent her a stern look.

"What?" Rachel said. "It's a simple question."

THERE WASN'T ANYTHING simple about Rachel's question, and she knew it, but the question prompted Graham to tug at the collar of his tux shirt, suddenly needing a little more air. Probably all those damn candles taking up the oxygen in the room, he decided. They'd been driving him crazy all evening. All that flickering made it difficult to carry on an intelligent conversation—especially with the way Courtney looked in the soft light.

He'd almost popped his cummerbund when she'd come downstairs with her hair up off her neck, her slender shoulders exposed, and that short dress showing him how long her fabulous legs really were. She'd looked so amazing all he could do was gulp.

"Well?" Rachel said now. "Since neither of you is going to answer me, can I take that as a yes?"

"It wasn't an appropriate question to ask, and you know it," Graham warned. "That's why we didn't bother to answer you."

She looked across the table at Courtney, then back at him. "Well, at least admit you think Courtney looks beautiful tonight, Dad."

"Rachel!" Courtney protested. "Don't put your dad on the spot like that."

But rather than have Courtney more embarrassed than she already was, Graham looked directly at her and said, "You look extremely beautiful tonight, Courtney. And so does my daughter, even if she is being a complete brat."

"Why, thank you, Graham," she said politely and picked up her wineglass. "I say we make a toast to your beautiful daughter, even though she is being a complete brat, for planning such an incredible meal for us tonight."

Rachel rolled her eyes. But she got the message from both of them to back off.

"To Rachel," Graham said, lifting his glass and touching it against Courtney's, then against Rachel's Sprite-filled wineglass.

But he hadn't missed Courtney's wink when their glasses touched, signaling she was pleased with the way they were handling the situation. That made Graham realize Courtney might be more of an ally than he thought.

Maybe Courtney would be a good friend for Rachel after all. He'd paused outside the kitchen on his way to dress for dinner and listened while Courtney patiently walked Rachel through making the sauce for the salmon. And as he'd entered his bedroom, he'd heard them laughing. He hadn't heard Rachel laugh like that in a long time.

Graham glanced over at his daughter again.

Seeing Rachel all dressed up made him wonder when his baby girl had grown into such a lovely young woman. But the dress she wore only reinforced Graham's belief that he was doing the right thing refusing to move to New York. Rachel had a lifetime ahead of her for party dresses and fancy restaurants. A lifetime where he would only be an afterthought, the father she might decide to visit now and then.

He'd wasted the first ten years of her life. He didn't intend to squander the short time they still had left together. And if that made him a selfish father, so be it.

Fathers were selfish when it came to their daughters.

Always had been.

Always would be.

"I want to make a toast to you, Graham," Courtney said, jarring Graham from his thoughts. "To you, for being a good sport and wearing your tux tonight."

Graham swallowed past his collar and bow tie again. The same way he seemed to every time she looked at him.

"You do look good, Dad," Rachel chimed in. "Even if you are forty."

"Hey, I'm not forty yet," Graham reminded her.

"But you'll be forty tomorrow," Rachel said. "And there's something we need to talk about before the party. I told everyone we'd invited a friend of yours from New York, but only Tiki and Gil know the truth."

"I knew Gil was in on it!" Graham complained.

"Not really, Dad," Rachel said. "I just made him promise he wouldn't let Courtney get back on the plane."

Courtney laughed. "And Gil sure kept his promise."

"So, let's just stick to my story, okay?" Rachel

begged. "No one needs to know the truth. I don't want Courtney to be embarrassed when she meets everyone."

It was Graham's turn to laugh. "And you being embarrassed over what you did has nothing to do with it. Right, Rachel?"

Rachel blushed. "Okay. I don't want *any* of us embarrassed. Agreed?"

Graham nodded and reached for his wineglass again. Besides, what choice did he have? At least they could get through the party and Courtney would be gone before Gil had the opportunity to tell everyone the truth of the matter. And Gil would make sure everyone knew the truth—the stunt Rachel had pulled was too sensational for Gil to keep quiet about it.

"Since I'll be so busy with your party tomorrow," Rachel spoke up again, "I want to give you your birthday present from me tonight."

And why doesn't that surprise me? Graham thought.

Rachel always knew exactly how to play him. Give the old man a present, and how can he stay angry?

His daughter was still smiling when she reached under the table and produced a small black gift bag with Over the Hill written across the front. "Happy Birthday, Dad."

Rachel slid the bag in his direction.

"You'll notice I'm ignoring the *over the hill* part," Graham grumbled as he unwrapped the present and pulled out a CD.

"It's a mix I made of your favorite Sinatra songs that you've bored me with my whole life," Rachel teased.

In spite of his irritation with her, Graham leaned over and kissed his daughter on the cheek. "Thank you, pumpkin. You couldn't have gotten me anything I'll enjoy more."

It crossed Graham's mind he hadn't used his pet name for Rachel in a long time. He was still wondering why when Rachel looked at Courtney.

"Dad's a closet romantic, Courtney. So don't let him fool you. He does have a sensitive side."

And then Graham remembered. His *pumpkin* could be downright *rotten* sometimes.

"Courtney's a big Sinatra fan, too," Rachel said.

Graham looked over at Courtney. "Really?"

Courtney shrugged. "What can I say? You can't grow up in New York and not be a Sinatra fan."

Rachel was out of her chair in a flash. She pointed a finger at both of them as she said, "You two stay right here until I get back. I'll only be gone a minute."

COURTNEY LOOKED at Graham when Rachel left.

"Do I dare ask what's coming next?" he asked.

"I have no idea," Courtney said, and it was true.

"Then maybe we should run for our lives," he said.

Courtney laughed. "Don't worry. Between the two of us, I think we can take her."

He leaned back in his chair and took a sip of wine, and all Courtney could think was how gorgeous he looked in a tux. And that led her to thoughts of how good Graham would look *out* of his tux.

Finally, she'd met a man who held her interest. And not just physically.

Courtney was attracted to everything about Graham. His intelligence. His wit. His quiet confidence. The love she saw in his eyes every time he looked at his daughter—

even when Rachel was being a total pain. If she could place an order for everything she wanted in a man, Graham would be the man UPS delivered on her doorstep.

How tragic there was nothing she could do about it.

Not in three short days.

Graham hadn't even known she existed until seven hours ago. Yet, he'd been on her mind for three long months. It wasn't fair to expect Graham to treat her like anything other than what she was—a total stranger.

A weekend wouldn't be long enough to change that.

But Courtney did hope one thing. She hoped Graham would at least think about her now and then after she was gone.

Rachel rushed back into the room holding a portable CD player, and two seconds later Old Blue Eyes was singing about strangers in the night exchanging glances.

"See," Rachel said brightly. "Even Frank is trying to tell you guys something. So be a gentleman, Dad, and ask Courtney to dance."

Courtney could tell from Graham's expression he hadn't seen that one coming. Neither had she. She was going to have a serious talk with Rachel about her constantly trying to push them together.

Courtney didn't want Graham to be forced into dancing with her, or *hooking up* with her, or anything else. She was still trying to think of some way to rescue both of them when Graham stood and held out his hand.

"May I have this dance, Courtney?" he asked politely.

The next thing Courtney knew, she was in Graham's arms. And her head wasn't reeling from just the fancy turns he was making as he twirled her around the great room of the lodge.

It barely registered when Rachel called out she was going to her room to call her friend Tiki. But the second Rachel left, Graham pulled Courtney even tighter against him.

She gasped, barely able to breathe.

He threw in a few more fancy dance steps as Sinatra sang "Under My Skin." Graham whispered against her ear, "Maybe Frank really is in on Rachel's conspiracy."

"Or maybe Frank's observing we can't dance much closer?" Courtney teased.

"Great comeback."

But he didn't loosen his grip.

That was just fine with Courtney. She hadn't been expecting this opportunity to be in Graham's arms. And even if it was only an innocent dance, at this point Courtney was willing to take whatever she could get.

When Graham curled her hand into his chest, Courtney rested her head on his shoulder. By the time the music track changed again, the song "Fly Me to the Moon" seemed exactly where Courtney was headed.

"I started reading your e-mails," he said.

Courtney pushed back to look at him. "I'm glad. I wanted you to see for yourself my only agenda in coming to your party was to meet you and Rachel in person."

He turned her into a spin. When they faced each other again, he said, "You mentioned you hoped we could become good friends. If you haven't changed your mind, I'd like that, too."

Courtney smiled. "No, I haven't changed my mind."

Graham pulled her to him again and continued to glide her around the room as if they were dancing in the grand ballroom of the Waldorf Astoria instead of a wooden-plank floor. When the song ended, Graham even leaned Courtney backward for a final dramatic dip. And he pulled her back up just as Sinatra sang about having a crush.

"Thanks for the dance."

"Likewise," Courtney told him.

He leaned forward and Courtney held her breath. His mouth kept inching closer and closer. Courtney was so sure he was going to kiss her, she closed her eyes.

"You know we have an audience, right?" he whispered.

Courtney's eyes popped open. "Of course we do."

They stepped away from each other.

"I really appreciate you helping Rachel with dinner."

"It was my pleasure," Courtney said.

He looked down at his watch, then at her. "You have to be exhausted," he said. "You're still on New York time. So why don't you call it a night?"

"I'll help Rachel clean up first."

"Thanks, but I'll pull cleanup duty. Just as soon as I get out of this blasted tux." He grinned as he unfastened his bow tie.

It was obvious Graham needed his space—without her in it. And Courtney understood that completely. She'd flown in from out of nowhere and landed right in the middle of his life. And though he couldn't have been any nicer under the circumstances, Graham had politely let her know this day was over.

"You'll say good-night to Rachel for me?"

"Of course," he said.

"Then I'll see you both in the morning."

But as she headed up the stairs, she took the words *good*

friends along with her. Graham had politely let her know not to expect anything more than friendship from him.

Too bad. Because she could still smell him on her skin. Still feel his arm around her waist.

And yes, damn him, she was still aroused from the feel of his rock-hard body pressed against hers.

For Courtney, that was a first. Usually, men bored her. Usually, all she had to do was look in their direction to have men falling all over her. Was that also part of her overwhelming attraction to Graham—his failure to immediately fawn over her?

Sighing, Courtney closed her bedroom door, unzipped her dress and walked toward the bathroom. She really was exhausted. With any luck once she hit the bed, she'd fall into a sleep so deep she wouldn't have bad dreams about those blank pages of her life that Graham was never going to fill.

She had a *friend's* birthday party to attend tomorrow. A *friend*, nothing more.

THE FIRST THING Graham did when Courtney went upstairs was walk over and shut Frank's big, fat mouth. He didn't need anyone pointing out how quickly he was falling under Courtney's spell. She'd felt so incredible in his arms, the only thing that had kept him from picking her up and carrying her off to his bedroom was knowing Rachel was watching every move they made.

Of course, Rachel was so determined to get them together she probably would have fluffed the pillows for them. His daughter was the real little witch in this situation: trying to work some mojo magic with her damn candles; carefully handpicking the right songs; forcing him to ask Courtney to dance.

Note to self, Graham thought. *Ban Rachel from watching romantic-comedy movies for life.*

The next thing Graham did was blow out each and every one of those candles that had been tormenting him all evening. Then he headed for the swinging doors that separated the dining room from the kitchen. But he didn't push through the doors. Not yet. He wanted to make it clear he knew his little witch had been eavesdropping the entire time.

"Good night, Rachel."

He heard her gasp. She popped out from behind the wall and stood staring at him over the top of the half doors. "What do you mean *good-night?* I thought you were going to help me clean up."

"I lied," Graham said simply.

"But, Dad," she whined. "That's not fair. I cooked."

"I cook every night of the week. And most of the time I clean up, too. So get used to it. Now that I know you have such a fondness for cooking, I'll be assigning both cooking and cleaning up to you from now on."

"And that's going to be my punishment?" she shrieked.

Graham said, "Along with doing *all* of the laundry. And cleaning the bedrooms and changing the beds after the guests leave. And anything else I decide to add to your new list of duties."

Rachel's mouth dropped open.

Pleased that he'd left his daughter speechless for once, Graham pushed past her, and headed down the hall to his own bedroom. He could hear her banging around in the kitchen as he undressed and got ready for bed. And though he did feel a little guilty for making Rachel clean up after cooking him that great dinner, Graham pushed that guilt aside.

He was tired of walking on eggshells around Rachel, letting her do as she pleased in order to avoid another confrontation about her returning to New York to finish high school. By his doing so, she'd had too much free time on her hands to plot and scheme and get in trouble.

Well, those days were over.

From now on he'd see to it that Rachel answered to him for every minute of her day. Never again would he give her the opportunity to breathe without him knowing exactly where she was and what she was doing.

Graham turned back the covers and got into bed. But as he reached over to switch off his bedside light, he accidently knocked the folder he'd left on his bedside table onto the floor.

Graham leaned over and picked it up.

And instead of turning out the light, he repositioned his pillows and sat up. Courtney said she'd given him her e-mails to clear up any doubts he had about her motives. Maybe finding out more about her was what he needed to get his own emotions in check.

Turning to the page where he'd stopped reading, Courtney's next words were:

Rachel told me how busy you are when you have a fishing party at the lodge, so please don't worry that she's bothering me when she calls at night while you're entertaining your guests. I don't have any siblings, so I've never had the opportunity to play the role of a big sister or an aunt. I thoroughly enjoy talking to Rachel. She provides me with a good excuse to take a break from this ad campaign I'm working on that consumes every second of my time.

Graham read through several other e-mails.

He learned that Courtney's best friend Beth had been living with her for the past two years after a nasty breakup with the guy Beth thought she was going to marry. And he knew that Beth was an aspiring actress, which meant she was between jobs more often than she was employed—another reason he suspected that Beth hadn't moved out into a place of her own.

The big shock, however, was learning that Courtney was Lisa Woods's daughter. The woman was a New York icon—with a past people found as intriguing as her accomplishments.

Graham had been hearing the story for years. How Lisa Woods had been disowned by her wealthy advertising king father when she turned up pregnant by a farm kid from upstate New York—a boy who was killed in Vietnam before they had the chance to marry.

New York society hadn't been shocked that a powerful man like Walter Woods would disown his disobedient daughter. The shock came when Walter died unexpectedly of a heart attack and left his entire fortune and his advertising agency to the very daughter he'd disowned.

The rest was history.

Lisa not only took over the agency, she doubled the fortune her father had left her in the first ten years. Today she was considered one of the most successful businesswomen in the nation. And she'd been featured on the cover of *Time* magazine to prove it.

Graham shook his head.

No wonder several of the e-mails mentioned Courtney being on the outs with her mother. Graham could only imagine what a woman like Lisa Woods would think about her daughter carrying on an Internet relationship with some hick from Alaska.

But did Courtney think he was a hick?

Graham didn't think so.

A woman like Courtney wouldn't have continued the correspondence without doing a background check first. When you had money, you knew who had money. And Graham's father had made his wealth in land development, so the family name wasn't exactly secret.

Is that why Courtney had made it a point to tell him who her mother was? Had Courtney wanted him to know up front that they came with similar financial pedigrees?

Flipping through the e-mails, Graham decided he would look for more minutia-type information about Courtney later. What he wanted to see was Courtney's initial reaction when she'd received Rachel's invitation to come to Alaska. He finally found the one he was looking for.

You aren't going to believe this, but less than thirty minutes after I learned I had landed the biggest account in the agency's history, I received your card and the invitation to your birthday party in the mail. I can't think of a better way to celebrate my success than by taking a break and rewarding myself by coming to Alaska. Thanks so much for inviting me, Graham. I'm really looking forward to finally meeting you and Rachel in person.

Graham closed the folder.

So, Courtney had told the truth.

Her only goal in coming was to meet them in person. From what he'd read so far, there was no indication Courtney ever had any starry-eyed notion about coming to Alaska for love.

Graham repositioned his pillows, placed the folder on his bedside table and switched off the light. But as he lay there in the dark, Graham kept waiting for relief to set in that the woman in his upstairs suite had never seen him as anything more than just a friend she'd met on the Internet.

Thirty minutes later, Graham was still waiting.

AFTER FINALLY CLEARING the table and cleaning the kitchen, Rachel was propped up in bed, the phone to her ear, Broadway curled up on the bed right beside her.

"And you really think your dad and Courtney like each other?"

"I don't know, Tiki," Rachel said, "but I've never seen anything so romantic. Dad twirling Courtney around the room in the candlelight. Them dancing so close together. Listening to the music they both love. And Dad actually dipped Courtney. Just like on *Dancing with the Stars.*"

"Wow," Tiki said.

"I could tell Courtney was completely into it," Rachel said. "She had this dreamy look on her face the whole time they were dancing."

"Falling-in-love dreamy?"

Rachel thought about it. "I sure hope so."

"Did your dad kiss her again before she went upstairs?"

"No." Rachel sighed. "He almost kissed her, but at

the last minute he changed his mind. But he kept smiling at her all weird like."

"Will-you-marry-me weird like?"

"I wish. Do you have any idea how amazing it would be if Dad and Courtney really did fall in love and get married?"

Tiki groaned. "Yes, Rachel, I know how amazing you think that would be. You could finally move back to your precious New York City."

Rachel frowned at her friend's snotty comment. But rather than give Tiki the privilege of being right about anything, Rachel said, "Maybe I would still want to move back to New York, maybe not. Courtney and I had such fun tonight, if Courtney married Dad I might not mind staying here in Port Protection until it's time to go to college."

Tiki let out an excited squeal loud enough to wake her ancestors. Broadway growled. And Rachel held the phone away from her ear until the ear-piercing scream ended.

"Okay, you've finally convinced me inviting Courtney was a good idea," Tiki said. "So what can I do to help you make sure they get together?"

"Well, I thought of one thing that might help the situation," Rachel said. "Are you sure you're willing to help me?"

"Totally," Tiki assured her.

"Great," Rachel said. "This is what I think we should do…."

CHAPTER SEVEN

WAKING UP ON HIS fortieth birthday to the smell of fresh coffee was a pleasant surprise for Graham—until he squinted at his bedside clock and groaned. It was only 5:00 a.m.

Obviously, Courtney was *still* on New York time.

But now that he was awake, he had to get up.

He'd never been one of those people who could lie in bed once he woke. It was lying in bed awake at night that had always been his problem.

Graham headed for the shower. Twenty minutes later he walked out of his bedroom and down the hallway to the kitchen. But instead of finding Courtney, all Graham found was his gurgling coffeemaker, the last stream of brew flowing into the pot.

He took a cup from the cabinet, filled it to the brim and took a long, welcome, wake-me-up sip before he pushed through the swinging doors into the great room. He stopped the moment he saw her through the lodge's front windows.

Courtney stood outside on the deck, her back to him, leaning against the railing and looking out over the cove. In a flash, another of his journal entries Courtney had saved came to mind:

There's something about standing on the deck at first light, sipping a cup of hot coffee and watching the early-morning fog roll across the cove, that has a way of making everything right in my world.

Except nothing was right in Graham's world at the moment. He felt as if he were free-falling every time he looked at Courtney. And when she suddenly glanced over her shoulder, held up her coffee cup and beckoned him to join her, Graham felt the floor disappear beneath his feet again.

He took a deep breath and headed in her direction.

They had another long day ahead of them. And who knew what Rachel was planning next? The only way they were going to survive any more of Rachel's pranks would be by keeping a united front—as friends, the way it should be.

Graham opened the door and walked onto the deck.

And he told himself it was only the caffeine making his heart race.

"HAPPY BIRTHDAY," Courtney said when Graham stood beside her.

"Thanks." He leaned against the railing, facing her. He took a sip from his cup before he said, "I did a little more reading last night. Congratulations on landing your big account."

"Thanks, Graham, I appreciate that," Courtney said. "Are you at the point in your reading where you're convinced I'm really not a crazy cyber-stalker?"

He laughed. "I never thought you were a cyber-stalker. But I was surprised to learn you were Lisa Woods's daughter."

"And I was surprised to learn that you were Grant Morrison's son."

"So, I assumed right," he said. "You did check me out before you continued e-mailing Rachel."

"Just being careful."

"As you should have been."

"I am surprised we didn't cross each other's paths somewhere along the way. I'm sure we know a lot of the same people. I guess it was our age difference that kept us out of sync."

"Ouch," he said, pretending to clutch his heart. "My age is *not* something I want to think about today."

"Sorry."

"I did meet your mother once. Right after college, I hadn't made my way to Wall Street yet, and I interviewed for a position with your agency. I expected to meet with some personnel assistant, not the legendary Lisa Woods herself. She completely intimidated me. Needless to say, I didn't get the job."

"That's my mother, the Queen of Intimidation," Courtney said. "She's so hands-on all of her employees have her handprint stamped permanently on their foreheads."

He leaned forward, pretending to examine Courtney's forehead. "What happened to your handprint?"

"Oh, it's still there. It's beginning to fade a little."

He looked at her thoughtfully. "I know what it's like to have an overbearing parent. My father wrote the book on the subject. And I also know how hard it is to break that hold. But if it's any consolation, Courtney, it's worth it. So don't give up on yourself."

"Thanks."

He turned to look out over the water the way she was doing. And as they silently watched the fog roll across the cove, Courtney realized all was right in her world—at least for the moment. She wasn't sure if it was the setting, or the man standing beside her.

Courtney suspected it was both.

"So?" he said, breaking the silence. "Any idea what Rachel has planned for us today?"

"Beyond me helping Rachel with the decorations for your party, no," Courtney said. "But I don't think we should let our guard down yet."

"My thoughts exactly," he said. "Maybe we should think about..."

His voice trailed off when Rachel walked out onto the deck in her pajamas, hugging herself against the chill of the morning. When she walked up beside them, she leaned over and gave her father a kiss on the cheek. "Happy birthday, Dad."

Then Rachel looked over at Courtney and said, "What's up? What are you guys talking about?"

"Just talking," Courtney said.

But Graham said, "We were wondering what other big plans you had in store for us so we could put the rescue squad on notice."

Courtney sent Rachel an apologetic look.

Rachel put her hands on her hips and said, "You want to know my plans? Okay, I'll tell you my plans. I'd hoped we could all go to your party tonight and have a good time. And tomorrow I thought Courtney might like to go out in one of the skiffs and take a tour of the island. And tomorrow night, I hoped you would fix Courtney one of your famous venison steaks you like to brag about. Is any of that too much to ask?"

"No," Graham said. "Those plans pass inspection."

"Good," Rachel said, hugging herself as she shivered again. "Then maybe we can all go inside now that you don't have to alert the rescue squad. It's cold out here. I'm starving. And Courtney and I have a lot to do before your party."

"I make a mean omelet," Courtney offered, trying to get back in Rachel's good graces.

Rachel's face brightened.

"Sorry, Courtney. But Rachel has been promoted to our new cook here at the lodge. She'll be making breakfast for us this morning."

"Fine!" Rachel snapped. "I hope you both like stale cereal."

Rachel stomped off, slamming the door behind her.

Courtney looked over at Graham. "Part of Rachel's punishment, I assume?"

"I might have to rethink that decision," Graham said as they walked toward the front door together. "If stale cereal is all she's serving, I'm the one who's getting punished."

"Does that mean you won't object if I show your new cook how to make an omelet?"

Graham grinned as he opened the door for her. "What do you think?"

COURTNEY FINALLY FOUND a cell phone signal on top of the ridge overlooking Port Protection. But she'd made the climb up the Stairway to Heaven with Broadway, not

Graham. Rachel had gone ahead to begin decorating for the party. And though Courtney had her doubts, Rachel insisted after Courtney made her calls Broadway would be able to lead her to the general store called The Wooden Nickel, where Graham's birthday party was being held.

Courtney found ten text messages waiting for her.

Nine were from Beth, dying to know what was going on. And in typical no-nonsense Lisa Woods fashion, the one text message from her mother contained nothing but a single question mark.

Courtney stared at the ominous punctuation mark mocking her, deciding she would deal with her mother later. First, she would call her best friend. She had far too much to tell Beth to put in a text message.

Beth answered on the first ring. "Please tell me the reason I haven't heard from you is because you've been in bed with Graham from the moment you arrived."

"The reason you haven't heard from me is the lack of a cell phone signal," Courtney said.

"And there isn't a phone at the lodge?"

"Using the guest phone downstairs wasn't an option. I needed privacy for what I have to tell you."

"Oh, goody," Beth squealed. "If you need privacy, the news must be steamy."

"You want the good news first?"

"Yes."

Courtney said, "Graham doesn't have a hearing impairment." Then she spent the next five minutes telling Beth the bad news about the big surprise she'd found waiting for her when she got off the floatplane at Trail's End Lodge.

When Beth finally stopped laughing, she said, "I'm sorry, Courtney. I shouldn't be laughing. You wouldn't be in this mess if it weren't for me."

"Don't be silly," Courtney said. "You were joking when you gave me the membership. I'm the one who made things serious. Besides, I'm not in any mess. Graham has been nothing but nice about the whole thing. And regardless of the situation, I'm still glad I came."

"True," Beth said. "You could have wasted another three months of your life on this guy. At least now you can come home, patch things up with your mother and everything will return to normal."

"I'm done with my mother's version of normal," Courtney vowed. "Being here has only reinforced that. When I get back, things are going to change."

"Oh, come on, Courtney. If you aren't careful, this war you're waging with Lisa is going to bite you in the ass. You're at the top of your career. And one day you'll be running the agency. Focus on that. End this fight with your mother when you come home."

"Good advice," Courtney said, "if I gave a flip about running the agency one day."

"Right," Beth said and laughed. "You work nonstop 24/7 because you don't give a flip about the agency. Good one."

"That's the problem, Beth," Courtney said. "I should have been elated for more than five minutes after I landed the biggest account in the agency's history. But I wasn't. I just kept thinking, now what?"

"But it's normal to feel a little let down after you reach a goal you've worked so hard for," Beth argued. "I felt the same way after I landed that part on the TV series that finally got me noticed as an actress. But after the letdown, you set a new goal for yourself like I did. And your new goal needs to be ending the quarrel with Lisa so you can move forward and set your sights on a larger account next time."

"Speaking of my mother," Courtney said, ready to change the subject. "Call her for me and tell her my plane went missing. You know she's never going to let me live this down, Beth."

Beth laughed. "I'll pass on calling Lisa. Anything else?"

"Promise you'll only buy me a card for my birthday next year?"

"Now that's a promise I can make," Beth said. "From my lips to God's ears, I'll never play a joke on you again."

"I'll see you on Monday," Courtney said, still smiling when she closed her phone.

But her smile faded when the phone suddenly came to life in her hand and she saw the number come up on the screen. Reluctantly, Courtney took a deep breath and answered.

"A simple reply to my text saying you were alive would have been nice," were her mother's first words.

"I was just getting ready to call you," Courtney lied. "I'm having trouble getting a signal here, and—"

"We have a problem. Jackson and Taylor have called an impromptu meeting."

Courtney tensed. The diet products company had announced they were going with her campaign only days before she left for Alaska. They weren't scheduled to sign the final contract for two more weeks.

"Don't tell me they're backing out," Courtney prayed.

"Not a deal breaker, just a few minor changes they want in the contract. The meeting is scheduled first thing Tuesday morning. Be ready to hit the ground running when you get back Monday night. I'll have my driver pick you up at the airport and drop you off at my apartment so we can go over the changes and strategize."

"Will do," Courtney agreed.

"I expected no less," were her mother's last words.

No "how are things going?" No "are you having a good time?" And definitely no "do you think you could really be interested in the guy you went to meet?" Nothing other than strict instructions to hit the ground running once she returned.

Hit the ground running.

Courtney felt like screaming.

So she did. Standing right there at the top of the Stairway to Heaven, Courtney screamed so loud Broadway threw his head back and howled along with her.

She'd been running to catch up with her mother since the day she was born. Yet she was always one step behind, never quite measuring up.

And Courtney was tired of it.

She was thirty-five years old, and her mother could still reduce her to a sniveling five-year-old. Why hadn't she had the courage to tell her mother no? That she wasn't going to come straight from the airport to her mother's apartment to strategize. That she was going to do the sensible thing and have the meeting rescheduled for Wednesday after she'd recovered from her trip and could be better prepared.

That's what she should have done.

Instead, she'd chirped "will do" like the faithful

minion she'd always been. Of course, she could always call back and tell her mother everything she should have told her before, Courtney reasoned. But Rachel *was* waiting for her. And poor Broadway still looked a little nervous after her angry primal scream.

Oh, please! Who was she kidding?

She could feel the fight draining out of her at the mere thought of saying anything like that to her mother. And once her anger made its last circle around the drain, she could feel the guilt slowly rising up in its place.

She'd been trying all her life to make up for being her mother's bastard child, as if that were possible. And maybe that's why she'd felt such an immediate bond with Rachel.

Courtney knew firsthand what it was like to be the object of a single parent's domination—the guilt and the desperation you felt for wanting a life of your own. Before she left on Monday, maybe she would talk to Graham on Rachel's behalf. Maybe it was time someone gave Graham a little insight on how daunting being the only child of a single parent could be.

In fact, maybe fate had placed her in this situation from the beginning, not to meet the man of her dreams, but to help a kindred spirit. And thinking of her kindred spirit now, Courtney looked down at the big dog patiently awaiting her instructions.

"Take me to Rachel," Courtney told Broadway.

Broadway barked and trotted down the stairs.

CHAPTER EIGHT

ON SATURDAY NIGHT, Courtney tapped her foot in time to the lively tune the small band was playing at the front of The Wooden Nickel. The building had originally been a cannery warehouse built in the early 1950s. Hal Dobson joked he'd named the place The Wooden Nickel because that's exactly what he thought the old building was worth when his wife, Peg, wanted to buy it.

But Peg had obviously been the visionary of the two.

They had converted the building into a general store, and Peg also ran a short-order grill out of one end of the warehouse. The large storage loft upstairs had been transformed into a spacious apartment that served as the older couple's living quarters.

A space this size in New York City would have cost a fortune to heat. But a large woodstove at each end of the warehouse put out enough heat that—according to the conversation Courtney had with Hal earlier—could run you out of the place even in the dead of winter.

Courtney fanned herself, thankful it was May and neither of those woodstoves was burning. With practically the whole town packed into the space for Graham's party, the body heat alone had the overhead ceiling fans running full speed.

Courtney applauded along with everyone else when the music stopped, and smiled at the two Barlow brothers grinning at her. The good-looking twins, Mark and Clark, were in their late twenties and talented musicians: Mark, a master on the banjo; Clark, a genius with the fiddle.

Though Courtney had no interest in either of them, the brothers had made it clear they were *very* interested in her from the moment she'd arrived at the party. Her gaze drifted instead to the far side of the warehouse—to the one man who did hold her interest.

Graham was standing by the pool table with his cue propped on the toe of his hiking boot, watching while his friend Yanoo lined up a shot. When the ball landed easily in the side pocket, Graham threw his head back with a loud groan.

Yanoo walked around the table, considering his next shot. He was a tall man, and lean, and he wore his black hair pulled back in a ponytail at the nape of his neck. Like Graham, he had a radio strapped to his belt, telling Courtney he was also a member of the local rescue squad.

Beth might have been joking about finding real men on the last frontier, but Graham and Yanoo were real men. They were the type of men who were willing to give back and take responsibility for being guardians of their community. So unlike the suits and ties Courtney came in contact with daily, men so self-absorbed and power hungry that giving back wasn't part of their vocabulary.

Rachel had been right, however, about Tiki's father being a man of few words. When Graham introduced them, Yanoo had said hello, nothing else. Courtney had caught Yanoo watching her several times, checking her out, sizing her up. Not that she blamed him. He was Graham's best friend. He had to be puzzled why Graham had never mentioned her before.

At least she'd be gone by the time Yanoo and everyone else found out the truth. And Courtney was thankful for that. She'd enjoyed meeting Graham and Rachel's friends. They'd made her feel right at home. She doubted she would have received such a warm reception if they knew the circumstances behind how she'd been invited.

And that thought sent her gaze right back to Graham.

If he looked any better, Courtney couldn't have stood it. Faded jeans. A red chamois shirt that made his ink-black hair look even darker. Shoulders so broad they should have been illegal.

He was all male and muscle.

All yum and no yawn.

Courtney fanned herself again and quickly looked away.

She searched for the little imp who had placed her in such a precarious situation. She found Rachel talking with her cute friend and Tiki's pretty mom, Hanya, who was an older version of Tiki with her dark skin and eyes and her exotic features. Hanya had been much more talkative than her husband. In fact, Hanya had seemed genuinely happy to meet Courtney.

"Enjoying yourself?"

Courtney turned to find Peg, a glass of red wine in each hand, smiling at her. Peg was still a beautiful woman, tall and slender, her snow-white hair wound into a bun on top of her head. Her eyes had a perpetual twinkle in them, and Courtney noticed they were the exact color of the turquoise jewelry Peg was wearing.

"Thank you, Peg," Courtney said, accepting the glass Peg offered. "I'm having a great time."

"Sit with me a minute," she said, pointing to an empty table not far from where they were standing. "I haven't had time to say more than two words to you all evening."

Courtney followed Peg, thinking that though Peg and her husband, Hal, were in their seventies, they were still full of vim and vigor and didn't appear to be slowing down one bit. Nor did their love for each other seem diminished in their golden years.

Courtney hadn't missed the open displays of affection they'd exhibited toward each other, with a hug here and a pat there every time they crossed paths in the crowd. She also hadn't missed the silent looks they gave each other—looks that said *I love you* without any words.

That was the type of love Courtney wanted someday.

A type of love Courtney feared she might never find.

"Rachel tells me you'll be leaving on Monday," Peg said once they were seated.

"Yes," Courtney said. "I only flew in for the weekend for Graham's birthday."

"I love Rachel and Graham like my own," Peg said. "And I'm so glad you came, Courtney. Graham and Rachel need someone like you in their lives."

Her comment caught Courtney off guard.

"I— Well, I certainly appreciate your vote of confidence, Peg, but I'm too far away to be much of a presence in their lives. And Graham and I are only friends."

"That's your story and you're sticking to it, right?"

"I'm not sure what you mean."

"I'm old, but I'm not blind, Courtney. You're crazy

about Graham. I see it on your face every time you look at him."

"Attracted to him, yes," Courtney admitted. "But I haven't known Graham long enough to be crazy about him."

"Nonsense. I knew I was in love with Hal the minute I laid eyes on him."

"And did Hal feel the same way about you?"

Peg shrugged. "It didn't matter how Hal felt. I knew he was the one I wanted. And I made up my mind nothing was going to stop me from having him."

"And you obviously succeeded."

"Of course I did. I simply let Hal chase me until I caught him."

Courtney laughed.

But Hal had walked up behind Peg just as she was finishing her sentence. "Are you telling stories about me again, my love?"

My love.

Courtney sighed.

Where Peg was lithe and thin, Hal was a robust man, not overweight, just big-boned and still rugged-looking despite his age. It had crossed Courtney's mind when she first met Rachel's adopted grandparents that she wouldn't have picked them out to be a couple. Peg was more refined and graceful; Hal unconventional, his gray hair trailing down his back in a long braid.

"I heard my name," he explained as he sat at the table with them. He sent his love a teasing smile when he added, "I hope you aren't complaining to Courtney like you have been to everyone else tonight because I won't take you to Seattle for the summer."

"For your information," Peg said, "I was telling Courtney I fell in love with you the minute I laid eyes on you."

"And made me the luckiest man alive," he said, kissing Peg on the cheek, then excusing himself.

Courtney looked across the table at Peg when Hal disappeared back into the crowd. "I hope you realize men like Hal don't exist anymore."

"Don't you dare brag on that old poop!" Peg warned. "I'm upset with him right now."

"About the trip to Seattle?"

Peg sighed. "Yes. Hal is refusing to take the summer off."

"You could always go without him."

"I could," she agreed. "But it wouldn't be much fun attending my fiftieth anniversary party without my husband."

"Fifty years," Courtney said in wonder. "You have my congratulations and my admiration. Not many marriages make it long enough to celebrate a golden wedding anniversary these days."

"I agree," Peg said. "That's why our kids insist on throwing us a party."

"And your children are in Seattle?"

Peg nodded. "Hal and I are both from Seattle. We moved here ten years ago when we retired from teaching. Our kids threw a fit, of course, but it had always been Hal's dream to live in Alaska. We spent one entire summer looking for a place to land. When we arrived in Port Protection, we knew we'd found home."

"How many children?"

"One daughter and two sons," Peg said. "And the

three of them have given us eight wonderful grandchildren. It makes so much more sense for us to go there than all of them trying to come here."

"If you don't mind my asking, why is Hal refusing to go?"

Peg rolled her eyes. "The store, of course. Hal doesn't want to close for the summer. Everyone in town would have to travel to Point Baker for all of their supplies."

"And there isn't anyone you could hire to keep the store open?"

"We've tried to find someone, but people in Port Protection make their living during the summer. Everyone in the job market already has a summer position lined up."

"Will Hal at least agree to close long enough to attend the party?"

"Yes," Peg said. "But I don't want to go to Seattle only for the party. We aren't getting any younger. We need to spend some quality time with our family. And you can't do that during a quick trip."

Courtney couldn't think of anything to say.

Peg's face suddenly brightened. "You don't happen to be in the market for a summer job, do you, Courtney?"

Courtney laughed. "I doubt Hal would hand the store over to a complete stranger."

"Hal wouldn't have any say in the matter if you want the job," Peg declared. "Besides, the store has never been our livelihood. We use it as a business expense to offset our taxes."

"Sorry, Peg," Courtney said. "I have a *full-time* job waiting for me in New York."

Peg reached out and patted her hand. "I was only half teasing, dear." But the twinkle in her eye was back when she added, "Still, it didn't hurt to ask. You know, in case you need a good excuse to stay in Port Protection for the summer."

"So Graham can chase me until I catch him you mean?"

"It's something to think about."

Peg gave Courtney's hand a final pat and left the table. Courtney reached for her wineglass. She couldn't keep from sending a wistful glance across the warehouse again. As if he could sense she was watching, Graham suddenly looked up from the shot he was about to make at the pool table.

He winked.

Courtney flushed hot all over.

"HAPPY BIRTHDAY!"

Graham tried to hide his grimace as Rachel and Courtney walked toward him, singing and each holding one side of a large tray filled with forty frosted cupcakes. The flames on the candles resembled a small bonfire, yet another reminder that he really was *that* old.

It took him three attempts to blow all forty of the candles out, but the crowd cheered for Graham anyway. And the minute the crowd descended on the cupcakes, Graham was wise enough to step out of the way.

Peg's cupcakes were famous in Port Protection and no one intended to be left out.

"Great party, huh, Dad?" Rachel asked a few minutes later, licking at the icing on her cupcake.

"The best party ever," Graham told her. "You really outdid yourself, pumpkin. On the decorations. The food. Everything."

"It's the least I could do for my tottery old father."

"And your tottery old father greatly appreciates it," Graham assured her, sliding his arm around his daughter's shoulder.

"Did you make a wish when you blew out your candles?"

"I'm well past my wish-making years, Rachel."

"I knew you'd say that," Rachel said. "So I made a wish for you."

She darted off before Graham could ask—not that he couldn't guess what Rachel's wish for him had been. And that knowledge caused him to look around for Courtney. He found her over where the band had been playing, flanked by the grinning-from-ear-to-ear Barlow twins.

She'd looked amazing in her little black dress the night before, but Courtney looked even better tonight in jeans and a pink sweater. *Hot* pink is what Rachel called the color, and this was one time Graham had to agree with his daughter's favorite adjective.

Hot described Courtney to a T. She was too hot to ignore, but too hot to handle. The exact reason why an old dog like him should stay out of the chase.

Plus, Graham wasn't willing to follow Courtney to New York City, and he was smart enough to know that's what it would take if they did *hook up* as Rachel so aptly put it. A woman like Courtney would never settle for a ho-hum life in Port Protection. Stalemate, because he'd never go back to a hectic life in the city.

Courtney reached out to wipe a bit of icing from the corner of Mark's mouth with her napkin. The poor guy melted right before Graham's eyes.

For one split second, Graham was jealous.

"She's beautiful, isn't she?"

Graham jumped at the sound of Peg's voice. "Who?"

"Don't play dumb with me, Graham Morrison. You were staring at Courtney as if you could eat her with a spoon."

Graham frowned. "You're wrong. It isn't like that between us."

"And don't give me that 'we're only friends' speech Courtney gave me earlier. A woman like Courtney doesn't fly all the way from New York unless she's interested."

"You don't know the whole story," Graham mumbled.

"I don't need to know the whole story. The way you two look at each other says it all. And if you're half the man I think you are, you'll do something about it before Courtney loses interest."

Peg walked off and Graham gazed across the warehouse again. Two other single men had joined her group of admirers.

His first instinct was to go over and rescue her, but Graham held back. It was already after ten and the party was breaking up. People were collecting their things, saying goodbye to their neighbors.

Besides, it didn't appear Courtney needed to be rescued. In fact, she seemed to be enjoying all the male attention.

Graham fought off another pang of jealousy and turned his back on the whole scene. That's when he saw Rachel hurrying toward him, Tiki right behind her.

"Tiki and I are leaving now, Dad. Peg said it was okay if I took the decorations down first thing in the morning."

"Leaving?"

Rachel rolled her eyes. "Dad. You gave me permission last week to spend the night with Tiki after the party." She turned to Tiki. "Isn't that right, Tiki?"

"Yes. I was standing right there."

Graham didn't remember Rachel asking any such thing.

And even if he had, things had changed.

"That was before I knew we were having a *guest* for the weekend," Graham reminded her. "Tiki can spend the night with us."

"But, Dad," Rachel whined, "Courtney won't mind if I sleep over at Tiki's. I'll go say goodbye to her now."

"Rachel come back here," Graham called out, but Rachel and Tiki were already running in Courtney's direction.

Graham swallowed, hard.

He and Courtney could *not* go back to the lodge alone.

Not when all he'd been thinking about all night was how much he wanted Courtney in his bed.

"SORRY," COURTNEY said after Rachel finished her sleepover speech, "but I think under the circumstances it would be best if Tiki spent the night with you."

Rachel's smile turned into a frown. "What's wrong with you and Dad? Are you *afraid* to be alone together?"

Graham arrived just as Rachel asked the question.

Courtney looked over at him. "Are you afraid to be alone with me, Graham?"

The look he gave her said he understood her meaning. "Nope. Are you afraid to be alone with me, Courtney?"

"Of course not."

They both sent Rachel a smug look.

"Oh, forget it!" Rachel huffed. "We'll go see if Tiki can spend the night with me."

When the girls walked off, Courtney looked at Graham and said, "I hope I didn't overstep my bounds by asking Tiki to spend the night."

"Not at all. I thought you were backing up my suggestion."

Courtney laughed. "If we both suggested the same thing, maybe Rachel's right. Maybe we are afraid to be alone together."

He didn't deny it—but only because he didn't get the chance.

Peg approached to give Courtney a goodbye hug. "Please come visit again soon, Courtney." Before she let Courtney go, she whispered, "And in case you change your mind, my job offer still stands."

Good lord, what was it with these people? Did they all have matchmaking on the brain? If she could have handled the embarrassment, she would have assured everyone she didn't need encouragement. She'd fallen for the guy already.

Peg pointed a finger at Graham. "And you. You remember what Mother Peg told you."

Despite Peg's insisting they didn't have to, they spent the next thirty minutes helping her get things back in order. On the way to the lodge—Rachel, Tiki and Broadway well ahead of them—Courtney said, "Am I wrong? Or was I the subject of whatever Peg told you to remember."

"No, you're right," he said. "Peg was trying to play matchmaker, too."

"I thought so," Courtney said. "Peg offered me a job for the summer running The Wooden Nickel."

Graham threw his head back and laughed.

His reaction ticked Courtney off a little.

"Why do you find that so funny?"

"You?" he said and laughed again. "Putting your career on hold to run a general store in outback Alaska for the summer? That isn't only funny, Courtney, it's ridiculous."

"Well, I disagree," Courtney told him, even though she didn't. Taking a summer job in Alaska or anywhere else was ridiculous. But it still irritated her that *Graham* thought it was ridiculous. That could only mean Graham didn't want her to stay.

He stopped walking and Courtney did the same. The dim glow of the solar lighting along the railing of the boardwalk gave her enough light to see his puzzled expression.

"You can't be serious," he said. "You'd really consider running The Wooden Nickel for the summer?"

"Are you implying I couldn't do the job?"

"Of course not."

"What then?" Courtney asked. "That I don't have the guts to call my mother and tell her I'm taking the summer off?"

Now he really looked confused. "How did this suddenly become about your mother?"

"Good question," Courtney admitted and resumed walking.

When he caught up, he said, "I upset you, and I'm sorry. The only reason I found Peg's offer funny was because you just landed that big account. Taking months off to run a general store seems ridiculous to me. That's all. It's none of my business what you decide."

Okay, he'd put her in her place. Though the fact that

Graham didn't care where she spent her time hurt a little, Courtney looked over at him and said, "Forgive me for overreacting just now?"

"Sure," he said.

They walked a little farther before Courtney said, "I guess when you mentioned my career, it reminded me how soon I have to go back to reality. It's been nice these past two days. No responsibilities. No fires to put out. No disgruntled clients. Right now running a general store sounds like a dream."

"We all have our dragons to slay, Courtney," Graham said. "Even here in Port Protection."

Courtney wanted to ask what Graham's dragons were.

But she didn't.

They walked in silence after that, Courtney pretending not to notice the full moon winking at them through the thick forest as they strolled along the boardwalk, or that the entire setting was achingly romantic. But by the time they reached the lodge, Courtney was grateful she and Graham had both insisted that the girls stay with them.

The girls would keep her from doing anything stupid.

There was no doubt in Courtney's mind that, had they come back to the lodge alone, she would have ended up in bed with Graham. And that would have been too convenient.

Her entire history with men had been based on the convenience of the moment and basic human needs. She wasn't proud of it. But she'd never met anyone who held her interest long enough for things to develop into a relationship.

The way she felt about Graham was different.

And reducing what she felt for Graham to a weekend

fling would have been far more tragic than never lying in Graham's arms at all. If she ended up in Graham's bed, Courtney would want it to be forever.

CHAPTER NINE

"COURTNEY? Are you awake?"

"Yes," she called out.

Graham didn't enter her bedroom. He only poked his head around the door. And wished he hadn't. She was still in bed, propped up on her elbows, looking straight at him.

Tousled hair.

Bare shoulders except for thin straps.

Sexy black lace barely covering her full breasts.

Graham almost fell to his knees.

Somehow he managed to say, "We need to get an early start if we're going to tour the island."

"Give me thirty minutes and I'll be ready."

"Do you want Rachel's stale cereal for breakfast? Or my famous pancakes?"

"What do you think?"

"Good choice," Graham said and quickly closed the door.

Seeing Courtney all mussed and sexy-looking took his thoughts back to last night. He couldn't help but wonder what might have happened if they hadn't thwarted Rachel's plan and left their fate to chance.

Don't even go there, Graham warned himself.

He no longer left his life to chance. He'd made that

change when he came to Alaska. Now he planned things out. That's what taking control of your life meant. And once he came up with a plan, he stuck to it.

Just like now, making sure Courtney was awake. The morning weather report called for afternoon showers, so if they followed his plan and left early, they'd make it back to the lodge well before the rain set in.

No one knew better than Graham how miserable it was to be caught out on the water in the rain. He'd made that mistake before. He didn't plan to make it again.

Unfortunately, living in the Tongass National Forest was always tricky business when it came to the weather. With an average rainfall of a hundred and twenty inches per year, rain could come at any time. Although the predicted high for today was in the mid-eighties, once the clouds rolled in, the temperature would drop like a stone.

So yes, planning was important to him.

In his personal life.

And also because of the business he was in.

He didn't like surprises. And maybe that element was another reason why the whole Courtney situation had thrown him off-kilter. Courtney had been nothing but one big surprise after another from the moment she set foot on his dock.

Walking home from the party last night was a perfect example. She'd been snippy with him one minute, and the next minute she'd been asking him to forgive her for overreacting.

He did admire Courtney's ability to admit when she was wrong. It was a trait Graham hadn't quite been able to master.

Of course, tomorrow morning Courtney would leave,

Graham reasoned. And then he wouldn't have to worry about any further surprises.

Or wearing a tux at dinner.

Or dancing close to Sinatra songs.

Or hot pink sweaters.

Or kissing her again.

"GO AWAY," RACHEL mumbled at the sound of the loud knock on her bedroom door.

Her dad opened the door and walked inside anyway.

Rachel yanked the covers over her head.

"You need to get moving," he said, "if we're taking Courtney on a tour of the island today."

Rachel pulled the covers down and glared at him.

"*We* aren't taking Courtney on a tour of the island today," she said. "I promised Peg I'd take down the party decorations this morning. Did you forget about that, too?" She elbowed the sleeping form beside her. "And Tiki's going to help me. Right, Tiki?"

Tiki only grunted at the sound of her name.

"I did forget about that," he said.

"Obviously," Rachel said, sitting up. "You have that scared-to-death look on your face again."

"I do not."

"Yes, you do, Dad. Like last night when you thought I was sleeping over at Tiki's. Why are you so afraid to be alone with Courtney?"

"I thought we cleared that up," he said. "I'm not afraid to be alone with Courtney."

"Then stop acting like you're four instead of forty. Courtney isn't going to try to make out with you, Dad. She doesn't even feel that way about you. She asked me after we got home last night to stop trying to force you guys together. I thought you would have figured out you were safe when she didn't want to be alone with you last night."

The tips of his ears were bright red.

That only happened when he was upset about something.

"I suggest you drop the attitude," he warned. "And whether you're going with us or not, I still expect you to be ready for breakfast in thirty minutes."

He walked out of her bedroom and closed the door.

Rachel crossed her arms in an angry sulk. At least her dad had given up on his stupid idea to make her cook. She just couldn't understand why he had to make such a big deal out of everything.

No wonder Courtney wasn't interested in him.

Courtney liked to have a good time. *Not* a good match for her dad's drill-sergeant mentality. And that thought made Rachel incredibly sad.

If someone like Courtney couldn't snap her dad back to his senses and make him see life was passing him by every day he remained secluded in Port Protection, no one could. And that meant she was right back in the same hopeless situation she'd been in before Courtney arrived.

Three more dreadful years, Rachel thought with a sigh before she nudged Tiki with her elbow again. "Wake up. We have to make an appearance at breakfast before we go take down the decorations."

Tiki sat up, rubbing her eyes. When she did, Broadway wagged his tail from the bottom of the bed.

"Did Plan B work?" Tiki asked with a yawn. "Are your dad and Courtney going alone?"

"Yeah," Rachel said, "but Plan B doesn't matter now. You heard Courtney tell me to stop trying to force them together. It means she's not interested in Dad."

Tiki yawned again and said, "Do you want me to ask the spirit guides for help?"

"You know I don't believe in all that spirit stuff, Tiki. But sure. Go for it."

Tiki assumed a cross-legged sitting position, held both arms out, leaned her head back and closed her eyes. A few seconds later, her eyes popped back open.

Rachel frowned. "That's it?"

Tiki nodded and uncrossed her legs.

"Well? What did you say?"

"I'm not allowed to tell a nonbeliever what I told the spirit guides," Tiki said with a smug smirk.

Broadway barked in agreement with Tiki's statement.

SO, HE WAS SAFE.

Good. Graham was glad. And after Courtney left, he wouldn't feel as if he were on a roller-coaster ride every minute of the day.

He had just finished placing the griddle on the stove and was busy stirring the pancake batter when Courtney appeared in the kitchen.

She was gorgeous.

Even with her hair still damp from her shower, wearing a simple sweater, jeans and very little makeup, she was beautiful. The best part was she didn't seem to realize it.

"That was quick," Graham told her.

"I hurried so I could help," she said. "While you fix breakfast, I thought I could pack a few things for lunch."

She walked to the pantry. "Is Tiki going with us, too? Or is it just you, me and Rachel?"

Graham quickly averted his gaze back to the pancake batter. "I'm afraid it's just you and me. Rachel and Tiki have to take down the party decorations." He finally looked up for her reaction. "That isn't a problem, is it?"

"No," she said. "Why would it be a problem?"

Right, Graham thought. *Why would it be a problem?*

Courtney didn't feel *that way* about him.

COURTNEY HAD JUST finished packing the cooler when Rachel stumbled into the kitchen with a surly look on her face. Tiki followed, trying to suppress a yawn.

Rachel looked at Courtney and said, "I'm sorry I can't go, okay? I have to take the decorations down."

"I'm sorry, too," Courtney said. "We'll miss you."

But Courtney knew the meaning behind Rachel's apology. She suspected the talk they'd had last night was a big part of Rachel's attitude this morning. Her big plan hadn't worked. And when Courtney left in the morning, Rachel knew any hope she had of returning to New York went along, too.

Courtney intended to have another long talk with Rachel later tonight. She wanted to assure Rachel she was not going to abandon her. She would still be only a phone call away. Their friendship was a bond Courtney wouldn't break.

Graham, however, was a different story.

Courtney glanced in his direction. He was loading the girls' plates with pancakes. After Rachel and Tiki headed through the swinging doors to the dining room, he looked at her and said, "Pray my pancakes do the trick. I'm still shivering from the chill in the room."

"I need to ask your permission about something, Graham."

He looked surprised. "My permission?"

"If it's okay with you, I'd like to stay in touch with Rachel after I leave. In case you haven't noticed, I adore your daughter."

He smiled. "I'd like that. In case you haven't noticed, Rachel feels the same way about you. She needs a woman who can be a good role model in her life."

Now Courtney was surprised.

That Graham considered her a good role model for Rachel was something Courtney hadn't expected. But she was flattered. Completely.

Graham smiled again when he handed Courtney a plate stacked with pancakes. Funny how neither of them mentioned keeping in touch with each other.

And why would they?

She would go back to her life. And Graham would breathe a sigh of relief that she was gone. Occasionally he might ask Rachel about her. She'd occasionally ask Rachel how Graham was doing. And all the rhetoric about being good friends would fall to the wayside the way most good intentions always do.

But today Courtney was going to enjoy herself. It was her last day before returning to reality. And she intended to make the most of it.

CHAPTER TEN

HAD ANYONE TOLD Courtney six months ago she would be spending a Sunday morning in Alaska, touring a secluded island in a boat called a skiff instead of taking a taxi to the Upper East Side for the weekly power brunch her mother hosted for the department heads, Courtney would have called them insane.

Yet, here she was—in her idea of heaven.

It wasn't just the magnificent scenery she was enjoying. It wasn't seeing all of the wildlife. It wasn't even the company of the man sitting behind her, skillfully steering the skiff over the dark blue water, that had her heart soaring.

It was the freedom.

The freedom to do nothing except fully enjoy her day.

Leaning over the side, Courtney stuck her hand in the water, letting the waves run through her fingers the way a little kid would do. What had ever happened to that little girl she used to be—the one who had her own dreams and ideas about what she wanted out of life?

It certainly hadn't been her ambition to become an advertising executive. She'd been perfectly content growing up on the dairy farm with her father's parents, and she'd thought her mother was content living there, too. But when she was eight years old, her life changed in the blink of an eye when the grandfather she'd never met left her mother the agency. The next thing Courtney knew, she was living in the lap of luxury in New York.

Courtney also hadn't expected that at age thirty-five she would still be single, still living alone and still have nothing to keep her warm at night except whatever new prospectus she was preparing for a client.

But what *had* her childhood dreams been?

Courtney couldn't remember. Childhood was simply too long ago.

Courtney screamed like a little girl, however, and jerked her hand in the skiff when a head suddenly popped up out of the water to look at her. Her reaction caused a loud laugh from Graham.

"It's only a nosy sea otter," he said when Courtney looked over her shoulder at him.

He turned the outboard motor off, letting the skiff slowly glide to a stop on the water. "We'll sit here for a few minutes until he loses interest," Graham said. "Sometimes curiosity draws them too close to the propeller."

The otter's head popped out of the water again. Now that she anticipated him, she was as excited as any little girl. "Oh, look at him, Graham," she said when the otter began an under-the-water, out-of-the-water dance all around the skiff. "Isn't he adorable?"

"I'll try and remember how adorable they are the next time one of the little rascals raids my shrimp trap," Graham said.

She was impressed with Graham's knowledge of the wildlife on the island. He'd given her the history of the sea lions they saw sunning themselves on the craggy rocks along the shoreline. He'd pointed out a Sitka blacktail deer and her triplets peering out at them from the dense forest, explaining how rare triplet fawns really were. He'd told her the names of more birds and waterfowl than Courtney could remember. And he'd taken her into a private cove where she'd been fortunate enough to witness a bald eagle make a swoop into the water, come up with a fish and fly off to its lofty nest at the top of a cliff.

Courtney was still watching the frolicking sea otter when Graham touched her shoulder to get her attention. He pointed out to sea. And that's when Courtney saw the large tail fin slap against the water.

"Amazing."

"That was my reaction when I saw my first whale," Graham told her.

The sheer enormity of the creature startled Courtney when the whale rose to the surface again. Images of Rachel's depictions of turned-over skiffs and spending eternity in a watery grave quickly flashed through Courtney's mind.

"There isn't any danger of that whale overturning us, is there?"

"No," Graham said. "We're too close to shore. The water's too shallow for the whale here."

Courtney relaxed with that news.

They sat in silence whale-watching for another fifteen minutes. And every time the V-shaped tail slipped beneath the water, all Courtney could think was how privileged she was to witness such a beautiful, untamed creature in its own environment.

"Hungry?" Graham asked.

"Starving," Courtney told him.

She leaned forward, reaching for the cooler at her feet. And that's when she felt Graham's hand on her shoulder a second time.

Courtney turned her head.

"Let's go ashore for lunch," he said. "I know a special place."

Courtney gave him a salute. "Aye, aye, Captain Ahab. Take me to your special place."

GRAHAM DIDN'T KNOW what he expected taking Courtney on a tour of the island. It certainly wasn't her excitement over the simplest things such as the sea otter. The reaction didn't fit with her classy advertising executive image.

Then again just when he thought he had her figured out, he realized he didn't know her at all. Unraveling the mystery of her was far more tempting than was healthy for him. As Graham steered the skiff into another secluded cove, he waited to see how long it would take her to discover why this place was so special.

He didn't have a long wait.

"A gazebo," Courtney exclaimed, clapping her hands.

Graham smiled to himself and aimed the skiff for the shore. He'd gotten permission from the Forest Service to build the gazebo for public use. It provided a place for the local fishermen to stop for lunch, and also served as a good shelter from unexpected storms.

He was pleased to see no one else was here making use of his special place. Graham told himself, of course, he was only trying to prove Rachel wrong—that he wasn't afraid to be alone with Courtney.

But Graham's ego knew the real reason.

He wanted to show off a little. And he wanted to see if Courtney was as impressed with his handiwork as she had been with the rest of the island.

The front of the skiff slid easily onto the sandy shore and Graham hopped out of the boat in his waders. Taking Courtney by the hand, he helped her onto the dry beach. After handing over the cooler, he waded back through the water to open the long storage box built into the side of the boat.

"Excuse me?" Courtney said when he pulled out the shotgun.

"Just a precaution," Graham told her as he broke down the gun for safety and propped the barrel casually across his left arm. "Most animals run the second they pick up a human scent. But we do have wolves and bears on the island. It never hurts to be on the safe side."

Courtney immediately looked to her left and to her right at the mention of bears and wolves. She waited for Graham to take the lead. As they walked up the long path leading to the gazebo, the only way Courtney could have gotten any closer to him was to climb into the back pocket of his jeans.

That made Graham smile, too.

And yes, dammit, his *male protector* gene did puff his chest out—just a little.

THE SURPRISE OF FINDING a gazebo in the middle of nowhere didn't compare with the gazebo itself. It was *huge.* Far larger than Courtney's five-room flat back in New York.

She peered around Graham's shoulder, admiring the enormous pine logs, the gazebo's bright green pitched steel roof and the way it was nestled into the thick forest like some fairy-tale castle. When they finally reached the steps, Graham closed the shotgun and propped it against the side of the gazebo. Courtney skirted him and walked up the steps alone.

Then she simply stood there, taking it all in.

The entire structure was pine. The wood had been coated with so many layers of polyurethane the interior shone like a newly sealed gym floor.

One continuous bench ran along the gazebo's circular walls providing enough sitting space for the town of Port Protection. There were also two long picnic tables made out of the same polished pine, one sitting to the left, and one sitting to the right.

At the center a large stone fire pit sat directly beneath the steepest pitch of the steel roof. And facing that fire pit was a giant porch-style swing fastened to the overhead rafters.

Courtney immediately wondered what it would be like to make love to Graham lying in that swing in front of a cozy fire. She quickly pushed those thoughts aside when Graham walked up beside her.

"I can see why this place is special," Courtney told him. "I've never seen anything like it. And I doubt I ever will again."

He only shrugged.

But Courtney could tell he was pleased.

"Let's take off our life vests and get comfortable," he said.

He walked across the gazebo and bent to slide open

a hidden storage compartment. When he stood, he pointed to the nearest picnic table and walked toward it with a plastic tablecloth in his hand.

"I keep a lot of supplies here," he said when Courtney walked over with the cooler. "Tablecloths, plastic plates and utensils, bottled water, a few pots and pans. There are also some blankets and matches for the fire pit. Things like that."

"You aren't afraid someone will steal your stuff?"

"No. People live by the honor system here. Whatever you use, you always put back on your next trip."

"The honor system," Courtney said. "Not a philosophy we practice in New York City."

He ignored her comment and said, "I also keep a woodshed out back."

He pointed to the right side of the gazebo. Courtney walked over and leaned out. As she expected, the shed was fully stocked.

"The other local fishing guides help me keep up the wood supply," he said. "Everyone contributes and pitches in."

"Is that why you made the gazebo so large?" Courtney asked as she approached the table to help Graham spread out the tablecloth. "Because everyone uses it?"

Graham nodded. "We've had as many as forty people stop here for lunch at the same time. The clients always get a big kick out of cooking their catch over the open fire pit."

"And the swing? Did you build it for Rachel?"

"Yes." He busied himself emptying the cooler rather than make eye contact with her when he added, "When I was a kid my grandfather built a swing like that for me behind the lodge one summer. The swing's been gone for years, but I never forgot it. I decided it was time for a new one."

"I think that's a wonderful tribute to your grandfather, Graham."

"Thanks," he mumbled.

She could tell he was embarrassed over sharing that piece of information.

And that's what she couldn't figure out about Graham. Why did he have such a hard time showing his emotions? She knew he felt deeply about life—his journal entries were proof of that. That's the man she had come to Alaska to meet. The type of man who could marvel at how remarkable God's gifts to man truly were. A man who took pleasure in sipping his morning coffee and watching the early-morning fog roll across the cove.

Where the hell was that man?

"Are you okay?"

Courtney looked up to find Graham staring at her.

"Yes. Why?"

"You're frowning."

"I have a bit of a headache," Courtney lied. "I always get a headache when I go too long without eating."

"Then let's take care of that," he said.

He reached into the picnic basket and handed her a sandwich. Courtney placed the sandwich on the table with the rest of their lunch—cheese and crackers, and apple slices.

Graham uncorked the wine and filled both of the plastic cups she had placed on the table. They sat on opposite sides of the picnic table, facing each other.

Courtney smiled and held her cup out for a toast.

Graham touched his cup to hers.

And that's when the downpour started.

"Good thing you suggested coming to the gazebo for lunch," Courtney mentioned.

"Yeah," he said. "Getting caught in the rain on the water is miserable."

THIS IS WHAT HAPPENS when you don't stick to plans, Graham thought, looking over his shoulder and scowling at the rain. Had he stuck to his original plan, they wouldn't have been this far away from the lodge.

He'd only planned to take Courtney on a short tour along the shoreline immediately around Port Protection and be done with it. But she'd been so thrilled by everything she saw, he'd gone farther east toward Whale Pass hoping Courtney would get a glimpse of what most tourists came to Alaska to see.

By then they'd only been a short distance away from the gazebo. And like an idiot, he couldn't resist showing off. He was no better than some teenage boy trying to impress his first crush.

It had been a dumb thing to do.

Now they would have to wait out the rain. In the gazebo. Alone. With thoughts he shouldn't be having, running through his head.

"Tell me about your grandfather," Courtney said, letting Graham know the only thing on her mind was conversation.

But Graham didn't want to talk about his grandfather. His grandfather had been dead almost twenty years, yet Graham still missed him every day. He usually got all choked up when he talked about him—the way he had a few minutes ago talking about the swing. It made him look like a blubbering fool—it was embarrassing.

Graham finally said, "Jonah Morrison was the finest man I've ever known. He meant a lot to me. And he knew how much I loved it here. That's why he left me the lodge when he died."

"And your grandmother Morrison?"

"She died before I was born," Graham said.

"My father died before I was born," she said. "But you probably already know that. My mother's scandalous past will follow her to the grave."

"I'm sure that's been hard for you," Graham said. "Never knowing your father."

"Somewhat." She smiled. "But not as hard as being left alone to deal with my mother."

"And your mother's the person in your life you've been trying to please?"

"Until now."

"I think most people grow up trying to please their parents," Graham said. "I know I did. Leave it to my kid to be the defiant one."

"Be honest. Aren't you secretly pleased Rachel has the guts to stand up for herself?"

"Of course I am," Graham said. "It tells me I'm doing my job. I'll let Rachel go when she's old enough to make her own decisions. But until that time comes, I'm afraid she's stuck with me."

"Rachel's lucky to be stuck with you," she said. "And when she gets older, she'll realize that."

Her comment should have pleased Graham. It only embarrassed him again.

Why was it so hard to take a compliment from her?

Was it Courtney's sincerity? That hint of admiration in her eyes? Or was it the fact that Graham knew he was a far cry from the hero Courtney had fabricated in her mind?

"Speaking of Rachel," Graham said, "I'd better let her know we're waiting out the rain. If I don't, she'll have the whole town out looking for us when we're late getting back."

He took the opportunity to leave the table and walk to the front of the gazebo. He unclipped the radio on his belt, punched the button and said, "Graham Morrison here. Comeback?"

"I copy you, Graham," a voice replied.

"I'm waiting out the rain at the gazebo near Whale's Pass. Can you call my daughter at the lodge and pass along the info?"

"Consider it done."

Graham clipped the radio back to his belt. When he turned around, Courtney was standing right behind him.

"Can we build a fire in the fire pit while we wait?"

The sight of her chattering teeth made Graham wince.

"God, Courtney, I'm sorry I didn't notice you were freezing. Of course we can build a fire. Let me get you some blankets."

She didn't object to that suggestion. Nor did she object when Graham told her to sit on the swing so she'd be closer to the fire. Within minutes after he handed over two blankets, Courtney was curled up in one corner of the swing and wrapped up in her blankets so tight, all Graham could see were two blue eyes peeking out at him.

She didn't emerge from beneath those blankets until he had a roaring fire going. By that point, Graham was relieved to see a little color coming back into her cheeks.

"Much better," she said, leaning closer to the blaze with her hands stretched out to soak up the warmth.

Graham was about to agree with her when the afternoon shower turned into a torrential assault so heavy the rain pounding against the steel roof was almost deafening. He cursed, jumped up from tending the fire and hurried to the front of the gazebo.

Another stupid blunder awaited him.

He'd been so eager for Courtney to see the gazebo, he hadn't taken time to secure the skiff to one of the five pilings he'd driven into the sand for that very purpose. The rough waves pounding against the skiff dislodged it from the sand and set the boat adrift.

"What's wrong?" Courtney called out.

Graham didn't wait to answer.

He had to act fast.

Jerking the radio from his belt, Graham tossed it on the floor. And taking a deep breath to brace himself, he ran down the steps and into the cold, driving rain.

COURTNEY JUMPED UP from the swing and pulled the blanket tighter around her shoulders as she hurried after Graham. It wasn't until she reached the front of the gazebo that she realized what was wrong.

Graham was in the water up to his waist, struggling to pull the skiff back to shore. Courtney was one second away from going to help him when he finally secured the rope over the piling. By the time Graham ran back up the steps and under the shelter of the gazebo, Courtney had the blanket off her shoulders, holding it out for him to dry off.

He wiped his face and shook the water from his hair

before he bent down to take off his wading boots one at a time. Water splashed everywhere.

"You have to get out of those wet clothes, Graham," Courtney told him when he straightened.

"I'm fine," he argued.

"You are not fine," Courtney retorted. "What you are is one heartbeat away from hypothermia."

Courtney turned her back. "See? I'm giving you your privacy. And don't worry. I promise I can control myself."

His voice was low and husky when he said, "Maybe you're not the one I'm worried about."

Courtney turned.

And hypothermia was the last thing on Courtney's mind.

They came together like an explosion, the kiss representing every ounce of pent-up passion they'd both been trying to suppress for the past forty-eight hours. Courtney was so turned on she could hear her own heart beating above the pounding rain on the steel roof overhead.

But as quickly as the kiss happened, it ended.

"This is a mistake," Graham said, pushing her away.

Spitting on her would have been more humane.

He stepped around her and headed for the fire pit. But Courtney remained where she was, too stunned to move. What had happened? How could he shut off like a switch? When she finally turned around, he was wringing the water from his shirt and his undershirt.

He placed his clothes on the rocks of the fire pit to dry, sat on the swing and put the blanket around his bare shoulders. When he looked up and saw her staring at him, Graham patted the place beside him on the swing.

As if!

Courtney was done. His tongue down her throat one minute. Calling her a mistake the next. Dammit! She had a little pride left.

"You think you have a clear picture of who I am," he said when Courtney made no move to join him. "That I'm the doting father and the grieving husband so devastated by his wife's death he was determined to keep his young daughter safe by moving to Alaska."

Courtney swallowed. The description was accurate.

"You're wrong," he said. "I was a rotten father and a lousy husband. So lousy I didn't even have the decency to care that my wife had been having an affair for over a year before she asked for a divorce."

Courtney closed her eyes. "Just stop, okay? I don't need to hear this."

"No!" Graham shouted, causing Courtney to jump. "You do need to hear this. You need to know the man you came to meet never existed."

He stood, his expression somewhere between angry and contrite. "The night Julia was killed, we fought. It was after midnight before I got home, and she was waiting for me. She told me about her affair and asked for a divorce. And to tell you the truth," he said, "I was relieved."

He sank onto the swing as though deflating. "Julia and I had been making each other miserable for years. A divorce would have been the best thing for both of us. But what made me furious was Julia saying she was giving me full custody of Rachel."

Courtney couldn't hide her shocked expression.

Graham's tone was cynical when he said, "Not exactly the reaction you'd expect from a doting father, is it?"

Courtney didn't answer.

"I knew Julia didn't want children before we got married. We both agreed not to have children. When she accidentally got pregnant, Julia blamed me for the one and only time we didn't use protection."

He ran his hand through his hair and sighed. "After Rachel was born, Julia's resentment toward me only got worse. We both stopped trying to make our marriage work, and Rachel got lost somewhere in the middle. Julia wasn't much of a mother. And I was a poor excuse for a father. But the thought that Julia would turn her back on Rachel as a way to finally punish me pushed me over the edge. I told her to leave. And the last thing I said before she stormed out of our apartment that night was that I never wanted to see her face again."

Seeing the agony on Graham's face was more than Courtney could tolerate. She walked over and sat beside him, knowing what was coming next.

He bent forward, elbows on his knees, his head in his hands. "I never did see Julia's face again. At least, not alive."

Courtney reached out and touched his shoulder for support, surprised when he leaned into her.

"The doorman and the two other witnesses on the street that night said it had all happened so fast. The car screeching to a halt. The young punk jumping out of the car, demanding Julia's purse. Instead of handing over her purse, Julia started screaming and hit him. The kid panicked and shot her in the chest. Julia died before she hit the sidewalk."

"I'm so sorry, Graham." What else was there to say?

He looked at her. "So that's the real me. A man so despicable he'd throw his wife out of their apartment at two o'clock in the morning without any regard for her safety. I live with the knowledge Julia would still be alive today if she hadn't been so angry with me."

Courtney started to argue. To remind Graham that sometimes bad things happened to good people for no reason. That in the heat of any argument, people said things and did things they regretted later. But Graham shook his head, stopping her.

"Go home, Courtney," he said. "What you're looking for isn't here."

He rose and gathered his clothes.

Courtney noticed for the first time that the rain had stopped. But her feelings for Graham hadn't stopped at all. If anything, the dragons Graham had to slay only made Courtney care more.

CHAPTER ELEVEN

COURTNEY WASN'T SURE how she'd made it through dinner Sunday night, but she had—for Rachel's sake. Graham had done the same thing. They'd both put on award-winning performances for Rachel's benefit.

But Graham had excused himself the minute dinner was over. A new fishing party would be arriving with Gil tomorrow morning when he came to pick up Courtney, bound for Anchorage to catch her flight to New York.

Graham had some things to get ready for his guests, he'd said. And maybe he did. But Courtney suspected Graham was using his guests as a good excuse to avoid any further interaction with her before she left.

And yes, that hurt.

But leaving her alone with Rachel to clean up after dinner was the perfect opportunity to have that heart-to-heart about staying in touch. Courtney didn't intend to waste the little time she and Rachel had left.

"I want you to still call me. Every night if you want to," Courtney said as she rinsed a plate and handed it to Rachel to dry.

"Okay," Rachel said, but with very little enthusiasm.

"And e-mail me, of course."

Rachel nodded as she placed the plate in the cabinet.

"That's what good friends do," Courtney said. "They make it a point to stay in touch."

Rachel burst into tears.

"Oh, sweetie," Courtney said, putting both arms around Rachel. "Don't cry. We'll still talk to each other. Just like we have been for the past three months. Nothing's changed."

Rachel pushed away from her. Courtney tore off a section of paper towel and handed it to her.

"You don't understand," Rachel said, dabbing at her eyes. "I'll never survive another summer here. You think I'm kidding, but I'm not. I'll kill myself first."

Courtney grabbed Rachel by the shoulders and shook her so fast, it scared both of them. "Don't you *ever* say that again. Suicide isn't something to joke about, Rachel."

"Okay," Rachel said, her eyes wide with fear when Courtney let her go. "I'm sorry."

"No, I'm the one who's sorry," Courtney said, pulling Rachel into a fierce hug. "I was your age when a good friend killed herself. And I've never forgiven myself for not taking her seriously when she said she'd never survive her parents' divorce."

When she released Rachel, Courtney said, "We all go through tough times, Rachel. But tough times always pass. Nothing is ever worth ending your life over. And if you're really having thoughts of suicide, we need to get you some help."

"Why can't you help me?" Rachel begged. "Ask Dad if I can spend the summer with you in New York. Please. I hate summers here. There's absolutely nothing to do. And Dad's always out with his fishing parties. I might as well be dead. That's the way I feel most of the time. Like a lifeless corpse, slowly rotting away."

"You know your father would never agree to letting you spend the summer in New York with me," Courtney said. "Besides, I work impossibly long hours. We'd never see each other."

Rachel's face clouded over again.

Courtney said, "Have you ever thought about asking Graham to compromise for the next three years and let you live in New York during the school term?"

Rachel shook her head. "Dad would never do that."

Courtney said, "You'll never know unless you ask, Rachel. And I hate to point this out, but the conversation we're having right now is one you should be having with your father. Don't be afraid to tell him how you feel about things. He loves you. He'll listen."

"Dad never listens to me," Rachel argued. "He only tells me he's the parent and I'm the child, and that's the end of it." She let out a sigh. "Can't you talk to him about us living in New York during the school year, Courtney? He would listen to you."

"I'm sorry, Rachel," Courtney said. "But you and your dad need to work your problems out together. Truthfully, it's none of my business. And it would only take about two seconds before your dad told me that."

Rachel's face turned blood red. "I thought you were different, but you aren't. And I thought you really cared about me, but you don't. So stop pretending you're so concerned! You just proved you're not."

Courtney reached for her hand but Rachel jerked it away.

"I do care about you, Rachel," Courtney said.

"No, you don't," Rachel accused. "You're just like my mother. All you care about is yourself."

Realization hit Courtney like a thunderbolt.

Rachel hadn't only been searching for a wife for Graham. She'd also been searching for a mother. Common sense told Courtney to back off. That it wasn't her place to step in and be a mother to Rachel.

The torment on Rachel's face wouldn't let her.

"What if I spend the summer here in Port Protection with you?" The words had popped right of Courtney's mouth.

Rachel blinked. "You would really do that for me?"

"Yes."

Rachel grabbed her in a bear hug.

This was a huge decision—a completely life-altering one. Part of Courtney was appalled at how quickly she'd made it. But another part or her had known she wasn't leaving Port Protection the instant Graham told her to go home. The scare Rachel had just given her only confirmed Courtney's decision that she wasn't going anywhere.

She'd come to Alaska to prove she could make her own decisions. And not her mother, or Graham, or anyone else was going to tell her what to do.

Staying was about what *she* wanted.

She wanted to see if she really could live in Port Protection without being bored in a week's time. She wanted to see if Beth was right, that the letdown she felt after landing her big account was only normal and that she would want to go back to New York and her career. She wanted to work Rachel's butt off all summer, so Rachel would never complain about having nothing to do again. And yes, Courtney wanted to stay and prove to Graham that his past didn't matter to her. If she left without doing all of those things, Courtney knew she would regret it.

She had a lifetime of regrets she couldn't change.

Courtney wouldn't allow that to happen to her future.

GRAHAM OVERSLEPT on Monday morning for the first time in years. He attributed such a sound sleep to his clear conscience over not taking advantage of Courtney at the gazebo, instead of the beer he'd consumed in his storage building behind the lodge while he was getting ready for his next fishing party.

He'd immediately excused himself the minute the venison steak dinner he'd fixed for the three of them was over. And he'd left Courtney and Rachel to clean up.

The silent ride back to the lodge after his confession at the gazebo, *and* trying to pretend nothing was wrong at dinner had been painful enough. Only a sadist would have stuck around to see the pity in Courtney's eyes where admiration had once been.

At least Courtney wouldn't leave thinking he wasn't man enough to finish what he'd started back at the gazebo. Now she understood he was man enough to let her go back to New York and find love and happiness with a man who didn't have so many demons in his past.

Courtney deserved happiness.

He didn't.

But another glance at his bedside clock made Graham wonder why Rachel hadn't already come to check on him. He rarely slept past six and it was now eight o'clock in the morning.

Graham also hadn't heard any movement in the

house since he'd been awake, leading him to believe Rachel and Courtney were sleeping in this morning, too. He'd shower and have breakfast waiting when they did get up.

He didn't want Courtney to leave hating his guts.

He just wanted her to leave.

For her sake, and for his.

When Graham made it into the kitchen fifteen minutes later, however, he found evidence that Courtney and Rachel had already eaten breakfast—two plates were stacked neatly in the sink, two juice glasses beside them. He forgot about making breakfast and made a pot of coffee instead. He had just poured a cup when he heard the front door open. Seconds later, Courtney and Rachel walked into the kitchen, Broadway right behind them.

"Glad to see you finally got up, old lazybones," Rachel teased.

The *old* reference set his teeth on edge. "I've been up. Where have you been?"

"Oh, here and there," Rachel said in a singsong voice.

Graham didn't miss the wink Rachel gave Courtney. If either of them thought he was going to beg for a more specific answer, he wasn't. His head hurt. He had a big day ahead of him. And he was in no mood for any more of Rachel's games.

Graham took his coffee, pushed through the kitchen's swinging doors and seated himself at the dining table in the great room. It was then he noticed Courtney's luggage already packed and waiting by the front door.

She obviously couldn't wait to be on her way. And he certainly couldn't blame her after he'd revealed that Dr. Jekyll did indeed have a Mr. Hyde side.

Graham had just taken his first sip of coffee when Courtney walked out of the kitchen and stopped beside him at the table. She was wearing exactly what she'd been wearing the first time he saw her. And those tight jeans tucked into her high-heeled boots still left Graham's tongue stuck to the roof of his mouth.

"I had Rachel figure up the cost of my plane ticket and my room for the last three nights," she said, placing a credit card slip on the table in front of him.

Without even looking at her, Graham said, "You know I won't accept this."

"You don't have a choice," she said. "I had Rachel go ahead and run it through on my debit card."

"Sorry, Dad," Rachel called out from the kitchen. "But Courtney insisted."

Graham's only answer was another sip of coffee. He didn't want to get into an argument with Courtney, even though it was obvious she was trying to provoke him. Besides, he could credit her debit card later.

What Graham wanted was for Courtney to leave on friendly terms. Then she could forget him. And he could forget her. And Courtney and Rachel could go back to corresponding on the Internet if they wanted. He only had to keep his cool and stay calm until Courtney left.

When Graham didn't say anything else, Courtney walked away from the table. But he watched her from the corner of his eye as she left. When he saw she was headed toward the front door and her luggage, Graham stood.

"Don't bother with your luggage, Courtney. I'll take your bags to the dock when Gil arrives."

She stopped and turned to face him.

"I'm not going with Gil."

Graham thought he'd misunderstood. "What?"

"I'm staying, Graham," she said simply.

Her words were still ringing in Graham's ears when Courtney opened the front door and took her luggage with her. Graham hurried after her. He caught up with her before Courtney started down the front deck steps.

"Why are you doing this, Courtney?"

She looked straight at him. "Do you have a problem with me staying?"

"I do if staying has anything to do with us."

Her eyebrow raised. "I wasn't aware there is an *us,* Graham."

"There isn't. And there *won't* be."

She shrugged. "Well, you know where I'll be in case you change your mind."

Her words sobered Graham faster than a face slap.

Courtney had basically just called him a liar.

And she was staying in Port Protection to prove it.

"I won't change my mind," Graham vowed as she headed down the steps, her matching pink suitcases in tow.

Courtney didn't answer.

And she *didn't* look back.

She left Graham standing on the deck, shaking his head in total disbelief. Rachel ran past him, hurrying down the steps before Graham could argue.

"I'm going to help Courtney get settled in at The Wooden Nickel," Rachel called over her shoulder.

Right behind Rachel trotted Broadway.

"Well, this is just perfect," Graham said, throwing both hands up in the air.

The woman he'd told to go home was staying. And his daughter and his damn dog were running off to help her get settled. Where did that leave him? As blindsided by Courtney staying as he had been by her arrival.

Graham stomped inside and slammed the door behind him. The very nerve of her. Telling him exactly what she knew would eat him up inside.

What a dirty, rotten, low-down thing to do to a guy.

He'd tried to do the honorable thing—warning Courtney he wasn't worth her time. Everything he'd told her at the gazebo was one hundred percent proof that there was no future with him—not now, not ever.

And what had Courtney done?

She'd ignored him completely.

Well, dammit, he wasn't going to be forced into anything. Not by Rachel or by Courtney. Courtney could stay in Port Protection for the summer or she could stay for the rest of her life, and it wasn't going to change a thing.

He was in control of his life now.

Making anyone else happy was *not* on his agenda.

CHAPTER TWELVE

AT THE WOODEN NICKEL Rachel helped Courtney put her things away in the guest bedroom that had been built in one end of Hal and Peg's upstairs loft apartment.

Rachel was so excited about her new summer job she could barely contain herself. And as thankful as Peg was for the opportunity to spend the summer in Seattle with her family, Courtney could tell Hal was equally thankful that Courtney had refused a salary. She'd told Hal instead that she considered spending the summer in Alaska rent-free more than a fair trade.

Courtney's only request had been that Hal and Peg would stay a few days to show her exactly what her responsibilities would be when it came to running the store. But as Hal had joked, the store basically ran itself. All Courtney had to do was be there to keep it open and keep the folks in Port Protection happy.

Of course, there was one person in Port Protection who wasn't happy. But Graham would have to get over it. She was staying. It was her decision. And as he'd been so careful to point out on the walk back to the lodge after his party, it wasn't any of Graham's business where she spent her summer.

Unfortunately, there was someone in New York who

would consider it her business. And when Courtney told that someone she was going to be one less vice president until September, Courtney feared her mother would *never* get over it.

But Courtney couldn't back down now.

She needed this three-month hiatus. It was a chance to figure out what she did want to do with the rest of her life. Maybe she'd go back to her old life. Maybe not. But at least whatever she decided would be her choice to make.

Courtney sighed and checked her watch again.

For the past thirty minutes she'd been sitting on the bed in the room that would be hers for the summer, holding Peg's portable phone and waiting patiently for the perfect time to call. Her mother ran her life with the same precision she ran the agency, and her daily schedule was as rigid as her office policies.

In exactly one minute it would be three o'clock Eastern time. That meant Lisa Woods would be at her desk, her afternoon cup of herbal tea in front of her, going over the daily reports she required from each of her department heads.

Courtney took a deep breath and punched in the number for her mother's private line. It didn't surprise Courtney when her call was answered on the first ring.

"Why does caller ID say you're still in Alaska?" her mother demanded without even saying hello.

"Because I canceled my flight this morning, Mother," Courtney said calmly. "I've decided to stay here for the summer."

The silence was deafening.

"And do what?" her mother finally asked. "Throw your life away over some man."

"I thought you would understand," Courtney said. "You threw your life away over some man once."

A sharp gasp was followed by her mother saying, "I was twenty and stupid! What's your excuse?"

"I don't need an excuse," Courtney said. "I've made my decision. I'm staying for the summer."

"What about your obligations here, Courtney? Do you really expect me to unload your responsibilities onto someone else while you take the summer off?"

"I haven't taken a vacation in years. I've earned the time off."

"Then don't expect me to hold your position with the agency until you decide to come home," her mother said. The chill in her tone would have broken a weaker person.

"I guess I'm your daughter, after all," Courtney told her. "I'm not backing down any more than you did when your father threatened you with the same thing."

A loud click ended the call.

Courtney sat there, feeling guilty for being so harsh with her mother, yet knowing she hadn't had a choice. The only thing her mother responded to was a blunt and to-the-point approach. Had Courtney started out with an apology, she would have been cut off at the knees.

A soft knock brought Courtney's chin up.

Standing at the door, Peg said, "Everything okay?"

"Yes," Courtney said, putting on a brave smile.

"Then let's go downstairs," Peg said. "I have a bottle of champagne begging for a good reason to open it. And I can't think of a better way to celebrate me going to Seattle and you spending your summer here."

Celebrate.

Courtney did need to celebrate her freedom from her

life in New York—freedom she hadn't even known she wanted until she arrived in Port Protection. Funny how spending time with Graham and Rachel had changed things, making Courtney realize how pointless her life had become.

Sure, she could brainstorm a new campaign. She could schmooze important clients with the best of them. She could even rake in a multimillion dollar account. But at the end of the day she still went home alone.

Would anyone actually miss her back in New York?

Even her mother?

Not really.

Life would go on as usual without her.

Even Beth, who had begged Courtney to stop being stupid and come home when Courtney called earlier to break the news. Courtney hadn't missed how cheerful Beth had become once Courtney pointed out Beth would have the apartment to herself for the summer.

Here in Port Protection, Courtney was needed.

Peg and Hal needed her to run the store. Rachel needed her to get through the summer. And Graham needed her, whether he knew it or not.

Graham needed her to shake things up. To get his mind off things he couldn't change. And get his focus on the things he could change.

That's why she'd laid everything right out in the open before she left the lodge. She wanted Graham, flaws and all. And she'd wanted Graham to know that. What Graham did with that information was up to him. But at least she was willing to stay and fight for what she wanted.

"Weakness is your worst enemy," her mother had always preached. "Boldness is your best friend."

She'd been bold with Graham.

And now she'd been bold with her mother.

One day maybe both of them would respect her for it.

RACHEL STOOD OUTSIDE her father's office Monday night, rehearsing what she planned to say. He'd been busy all afternoon with his new guests. But now dinner was over, she'd cleaned up the kitchen, and the guests had all gone upstairs to bed.

His office door was open, and Rachel had been standing there long enough for him to notice. The fact he was ignoring her on purpose confirmed what Rachel already suspected. Her dad was *not* pleased about Courtney staying in Port Protection for the summer.

Well, too bad for him.

Rachel was thrilled. Her problem was going to be getting her dad to agree she could start working for Courtney at the store next week when school let out.

Rachel cleared her throat. Her dad still refused to look up. She walked into his office anyway.

"I need to talk to you for a minute, Dad."

He finally leaned back in his chair, staring at her. "If what you have to say has anything to do with Courtney, I'm not interested."

Rachel didn't intend to be put off. "It's more about me than it is about Courtney. She offered me a job at The Wooden Nickel. I really want to do that, Dad."

"And what about your job here?" he reminded her. "Did you forget the new responsibilities you've acquired as part of the punishment I promised you?"

"No, I didn't forget," Rachel said. "I can keep up with all the laundry and clean the bedrooms and change the sheets in the morning when we have guests. And I can work for Courtney in the afternoons. And on the days when we don't have guests, I can work whenever Courtney needs me."

"That's a busy schedule, Rachel."

"That's the whole idea, Dad. You know how much I hate having nothing to do in the summer. It makes me crazy."

He looked at her a few seconds more before he said, "Your chores here come first. As long as you remember that, you can work for Courtney if you want."

"Sweet," Rachel said. "Thanks, Dad."

She couldn't believe it had been so easy. Because, honestly, she'd expected a flat-out no.

She'd obviously caught him in a good mood. And since her father was being agreeable at the moment, Rachel decided to run something else by him that she wanted to do.

"If it's okay, I also want Broadway to stay with Courtney for the summer. I think she'll feel safer at night with him there for protection."

He laughed. "And how do you plan to accomplish that? Broadway isn't going to stay with Courtney. Not unless you chain him."

Rachel gasped. "I'd never chain Broadway. And he will stay with Courtney, Dad. We've already had a long talk about it. Broadway understands. He'll do whatever I tell him."

"Twenty bucks says Broadway will beat you back home the second you try to leave him."

"Make it one hundred bucks and you have a deal."

"You don't have one hundred dollars, Rachel."

Rachel grinned. "I will when I win the bet."

She leaned across his desk with her hand out. They shook on the deal. "I love you, Dad. And I'm really glad you aren't acting like a jerk because Courtney's staying."

"Why would I act like a jerk? It's nothing to me if Courtney stays."

"I know," Rachel said, "but I'm still glad you aren't acting all weird like. I know things didn't go well when you took her on the tour of the island."

He sat straight up in his chair. "Did Courtney tell you that?"

"No. But I'm not stupid. I knew something was wrong the minute you guys got back."

He shook his head. "You're mistaken. Nothing went wrong."

"Yeah, that's what Courtney said, too. That's why I don't believe either of you."

He frowned. "Do you want to work for Courtney this summer?"

Rachel rolled her eyes. "You know I do."

He pointed to the door. "Then let me get some work done before I change my mind. I have an early day tomorrow."

Rachel knew better than to push him. She blew him a kiss and left his office. She didn't care what her Dad or Courtney claimed. Something had happened between them when they were alone on Sunday.

Rachel hoped whatever the big deal between them was, it wouldn't keep them from becoming closer over the summer. Now that Courtney was staying, Rachel wasn't going to give up the idea that her dad and Courtney would somehow fall in love and get married. And if they did, Rachel wouldn't even care if they never moved back to New York City—she'd still have a mom.

A mom she could talk to about anything.

A mom who really listened to her.

And a mom who already cared more about her than her real mother ever had.

AFTER RACHEL LEFT his office, Graham leaned back in his chair again, knowing he'd done the right thing by allowing Rachel to work for Courtney over the summer. After all, hadn't he agreed that Courtney could continue her friendship with Rachel after she left?

Still, Courtney staying meant he'd have to keep his guard up at all times. Graham wanted Courtney as much as he didn't. If that made any sense.

When he thought about it, he decided maybe this situation was better for both of them. There wouldn't be any doubts now. Courtney would see he was right and realize how ill-suited she was for a life in secluded Port Protection. And he wouldn't spend the rest of his life wondering if he'd made a big mistake by not asking her to stay.

He would make sure never to be alone with her again. Not under any circumstances.

But Graham would keep an eye on her. Rachel was responsible for Courtney coming to Port Protection. And according to her own words, he was responsible for Courtney staying.

That meant Graham had an obligation to ensure nothing happened to Courtney. Whether she believed it or not, living in the wilds of Alaska wasn't easy. You had to stay on your toes. You had to stay aware of your surroundings. And you had to be prepared to defend yourself against the elements and the wildlife, if necessary.

There were other dangers just as serious.

When word spread that a sexy single blonde was running The Wooden Nickel for the summer, every single man on the island would make it a point to pay a visit to Port Protection. Courtney was going to need someone to watch her back, keep her safe from the riffraff that came knocking on her door.

Graham was the only man for the job.

But he'd stay in the background where he belonged.

While out on the water today, he'd had a lot of time to think. Him alone in one skiff, guiding his three guests from Idaho in another skiff to the best fishing spots. He'd come to the conclusion that as long as he remained indifferent to Courtney, she'd eventually give up her notion that he was going to change his mind.

He wouldn't be rude. And he wouldn't be a jerk as Rachel had feared.

He'd simply be himself—*not* interested.

CHAPTER THIRTEEN

HER ABILITY TO be bold, Courtney decided, didn't mean jack when it came to machinery. She'd been bold all morning. And as she rummaged through Hal's toolbox, Courtney couldn't help but wish they'd had more than a week together before Peg and Hal left.

The generator was out—again. But this time she couldn't get it started.

She'd briefly thought of calling Graham. The only time Courtney had seen Graham since leaving the lodge was two weeks ago when he'd arrived at The Wooden Nickel to say goodbye to Peg and Hal. He'd been polite, but he'd basically ignored her.

So, no. She was not calling Graham for help.

It didn't matter that Rachel had told her Graham's schedule had been filled with back-to-back fishing parties. He was trying to prove a point by avoiding her, and Courtney knew it. Whether she'd stayed in Port Protection or not, Graham was making it clear that he *still* wasn't interested.

But summer wasn't over. And Graham couldn't avoid her forever.

Courtney gave another bold turn with the wrench she was holding. And another. Still, the bolt didn't budge.

She finally looked over at Broadway, who'd been sitting beside her the entire time. "You realize we're running out of wrenches. Right?"

Broadway whined before he suddenly bounded off.

Courtney let out a sigh and turned her attention back to the generator. She pulled another weapon of choice out of Hal's toolbox. When the wrench still didn't fit, Courtney banged it against the bolt.

"I hate you, hate you, *hate* you!"

"Are you talking to me, or the generator?"

Courtney popped up from her crouched position.

Graham was staring at her, Broadway right beside him.

Crap. Why did he have to show up *now?*

She didn't want Graham gloating over her not being able to fix the generator. And she definitely didn't want him seeing her like this, wearing one of Hal's old shirts she had taken from the rag bin, a pair of dirty sweats and with a smear of grease across her brow from when she'd dragged her arm across her forehead earlier to push her hair out of her eyes.

"Need some help?" he asked, stating the obvious.

Courtney wanted to tell him not just no, but hell no.

But she wasn't stupid.

"I think the fuel valve's clogged."

She stood behind Graham, peering over his shoulder and watching every move he made. She took note of the wrench he used, and the way he loosened the valve which happened to be the opposite way from how she was trying to loosen the blasted thing. And when he removed the valve and tapped it against the ground to clean it, Courtney made a note of that, too.

After Graham replaced the valve, he walked over to

the breaker box and flipped the switch. He seemed pleased when the generator instantly came to life and started purring like a kitten.

"Thanks."

"No problem," he said. "I stopped by to tell you it's going to be after lunch before Rachel can come to work today. Our guests left this morning, so she's got extra chores. She tried to call earlier, but..." His voice trailed off as he purposely looked at the generator, then back at her.

"No problem," Courtney said, stealing his own line.

"*And*," he added as he took a slip of paper from his shirt pocket, "Peg always makes up my grocery order for me. Since you're going to be shorthanded, I thought you might want to get an early start before the lunch crowd shows up. I'll stop by for those things later on my way home from Point Baker."

Courtney accepted Graham's list. She didn't comment on the fact that since his guests had already left, it would have been nice if he'd allowed Rachel to work during the busiest part of the day when customers dropped by for a hot dog or a burger from the short-order grill, then finish her chores at the lodge later. Nor did she point out that, regardless of the arrangement he had with Peg, she *wasn't* Peg. And even though Courtney had to bite her tongue to keep from saying it, she also didn't tell Graham that for the rest of the summer he could get his own grocery order together—she wasn't his damn maid.

She simply wouldn't give Graham that satisfaction. Instead she said, "I'll have everything ready."

"Wonderful."

"Glad you think so."

"I wasn't trying to be smart about it, Courtney."

"Nor was I, Graham."

"Is this the way it's going to be between us?"

Courtney feigned surprise. "I have no idea what you mean."

He frowned. "I think you know exactly what I mean."

Courtney crossed her arms. "Well, I'm sorry, but you're wrong."

"I'm talking about this whole friction thing that seems to be developing between us," he explained. "I'd hoped we would be mature enough to skip all that."

"I couldn't agree more. And to prove it, I'll fix dinner for you and Rachel tomorrow night. Seven-thirty okay?"

The look on his face was priceless.

He stalled for a second before he said, "I have a rescue squad meeting this Saturday night. But you're welcome to come to the lodge and have dinner with us tonight if you want."

"Sorry," Courtney said. "I already have plans."

She could tell he wanted to ask with whom.

"Some other time, then," he said.

"Definitely."

He turned and walked away.

"You will be back by six, right?" Courtney called out.

Graham turned back around. "Why six? The store doesn't close until seven."

"Tonight I'm closing at six," Courtney said with authority. "I have plans, remember?"

"If I'm not back, I'll pick up my order tomorrow," was all he said.

When Graham disappeared around the side of the

building, Courtney smiled. He'd be back at six. She'd bet money on it. And when he did come back for his groceries, she didn't intend to look like some grease monkey.

GRAHAM HOPPED INTO the skiff and eased away from the dock below The Wooden Nickel, trying to get his blood pressure under control. Damn, but Courtney was exasperating. And she was also so damn cute it irritated him.

When he'd found her crouched down behind the generator, she'd looked like a genie popping up out of a bottle. Except maybe for that grease smudge across her forehead.

And talk about quarrelsome. You could probably open the dictionary and find her smiling face right next to that word. Yeah, she was scrappy, all right. Too scrappy for him.

Graham didn't like controversy.

He liked to live and let live. No drama. No one person always trying to outwit the other. Just plain old peace and solitude. That's the life he wanted. And he didn't give a flip about Courtney's Friday-night plans.

He was glad she had plans. He hoped she had plans every night of the week. The busier she stayed, the less trouble for him.

But the longer he thought about Courtney's plans, the tighter Graham's grip got around the throttle. Before he realized it, the skiff was bouncing along on top of the water like a supercharged Jet Ski.

Graham eased up on the throttle. Any other time he would have been soaking up such a glorious day like a thirsty sponge. Yet today the brilliant sunlight dancing across the water only reminded him of the highlights in Courtney's hair.

Who was he kidding?

There were few hours in the day that he *didn't* think about Courtney. Of course, he had himself to thank for that, reading all those damn e-mails.

He should have known better.

He didn't need to know the intimate details about Courtney that she'd e-mailed in her top ten favorites list. Such as fall being her favorite time of year. Fall had always been his favorite time of year, too. Now he'd think of her every time the damn season rolled around.

She'd also stolen his pleasure over having a white Christmas for the rest of his life. And he'd never be able to look at peanut butter again without thinking about how Courtney loved to eat it straight from the jar.

He wouldn't let himself think about a hot bubble bath being number one on her list of favorite things. If he let himself think about that, he'd be reminded of Peg and Hal's old-fashioned bathtub with the big claw feet. And that would only lead to thoughts of Courtney sitting in that tub *naked.*

Thoughts like those would drive any man insane.

Insanity, Graham thought and frowned. He'd been teetering on the edge of insanity from the moment Courtney stepped off the plane. He needed to get himself grounded again. And with that thought in mind, Graham throttled the motor down on low as he approached the fifth cove past The Wooden Nickel.

He'd make a stop before going to Point Baker. See the one person who could get him grounded again.

Graham steered the skiff into the cove and toward the

dock in the distance. When he got closer, he could see Yanoo standing outside his workshop a few yards below his house. One of Yanoo's skiffs was up on sawhorses. His best friend was busy sanding the bottom of the boat.

Brothers in spirit.

That's what his grandfather had called them when Graham and Yanoo were boys. They'd been joined at the hip, running loose on the island and loving every minute of it.

They were still brothers in spirit, which was the reason Graham was pulling up to Yanoo's dock now.

Yanoo's wife waved from her doorway when Graham climbed up on the dock. Graham waved back, and was glad when Hanya walked inside the house instead of approaching to chat. As much as Graham loved Hanya, what he needed right now was man talk.

Straight man talk.

Yanoo saw him coming, put down the sandpaper and took off his work gloves. He went into the workshop, then shortly emerged with a thermos in one hand, two cups in the other. Yanoo handed Graham a cup, unscrewed the top of the thermos and poured coffee for them.

"Fishing's been good this week, I hear," Yanoo said.

"Yeah, I had a good week and my guests went home happy. You can't ask for much more than that."

"Now you're the only fish left on the hook."

And that's why they were brothers in spirit. Without asking, Yanoo knew why Graham had come.

"I'm *not* on the hook."

"Yet," Yanoo said. "I've seen the bait."

"That's my problem."

"Maybe she's your solution."

Graham frowned. "To what?"

"The emptiness you brought back with you," Yanoo said.

Not the straight talk Graham wanted.

"That's why I need to leave her alone. Courtney didn't stay to have some summer fling. She wants what I can't give her."

Yanoo took a sip from his cup. "Can't give her? Or won't give her?"

"Can't. Won't. Same thing."

"I like her."

Graham laughed. "You don't even know her."

"Hanya invited her to dinner last week," Yanoo said. "It gave me a chance to get to know her."

"And what did you like so much about her?"

"Her staying means she can see through your bullshit."

"Whose side are you on?"

"I remember asking you the same thing about fifteen years ago," Yanoo reminded him.

"That was different. You'd been in love with Hanya since we were kids. You were just too ornery and stubborn to admit it. And you almost lost her in the process."

"Then I'll tell you what you told me then. If you make the wrong decision, don't whine about it later."

"Have you ever known me to whine about anything, Yanoo?"

"No. You like to suffer in silence."

Graham tossed the coffee onto the ground and handed Yanoo his cup, signaling this discussion was over. He'd come for support. Not a lecture. And if he preferred to suffer in silence, it was nobody's damn business but his own.

"I'll see you later," Graham called over his shoulder as he headed back toward the dock.

Yanoo comparing his relationship with Hanya to the situation with Courtney was just plain stupid. Graham had known Courtney, what? A little over two weeks now? You didn't fall in love with someone in two weeks' time.

He was attracted to her, yes.

In love with her, no.

He wasn't capable of falling in love.

And that wasn't bullshit.

COURTNEY LOOKED AT herself one last time in Peg's full-length bathroom mirror, then looked down at Broadway, who was sitting beside her as usual. "Okay," she said to her new best friend. "Is what I'm wearing too much?"

Broadway's whine was rather mournful.

"Oh, what do you know," Courtney grumbled. "You have one blue eye and one brown eye. I'm pretty sure that disqualifies you as any kind of fashion expert."

Okay, so maybe the short white jacket and the low-cut red camisole were a bit much for Port Protection. But they dressed up her jeans perfectly. And so did the red sling-back pumps she was wearing that also weren't the norm in her new locale.

Courtney didn't care.

She liked the look and she was wearing it.

Besides, she'd ordered a ton of other stuff online that was suitable for her summer in Alaska, and she'd paid exorbitant postage fees to have those things express mailed. She now had a pair of sensible hiking boots. She'd purchased khaki pants and long-sleeved shirts to keep the bugs away. She'd gone all out in the rain gear department. She'd even purchased several pairs of flannel pajamas—a first—since even in June the nights were chilly in Port Protection.

Of course, she'd also ordered a few things that weren't within the sensible realm for her new lifestyle. Like the ton of sexy new underwear she absolutely refused to do without regardless of where she was living. And there were a few sexier-style tops and jackets like the outfit she was wearing now.

Did her new outfit show her every curve?

You betcha! Courtney thought with a smile.

And when Graham finally showed up for his supplies, she hoped he noticed she had a body made for more than gathering up his grocery order.

Broadway's ears perked.

Seconds later, the bell on the front door sounded below. When the husky left the bathroom, Courtney glanced in the mirror one last time.

"Hey, big fellow," she heard Graham say as she walked toward the spiral staircase that led from the loft down to the store.

Chin up. Boobs out. Stomach in.

Courtney started down the stairs. When she reached the lower level, however, Graham's reaction wasn't what she'd hoped for. He barely even looked in her direction. Instead, he headed for the five large sacks she had waiting for him on the counter next to the cash register.

"All ready and waiting," Courtney told him cheerfully.

"Thanks," he mumbled when she walked up beside him. "You do know the importance of using the incinerator daily, don't you?"

The incinerator?

Was he kidding?

She was standing here, looking pretty hot if she had to say so herself, and all Graham wanted to know was if she used the incinerator daily. Unbelievable.

"Yes, Graham," Courtney said. "I know the importance of using the incinerator daily."

"Good," he said. "Even one scrap of garbage left overnight can attract the kind of customers you don't want hanging around here."

Courtney folded her arms across her chest—the chest Graham *wasn't* looking at. "Got it," she said.

He frowned. "If you think I'm joking, I'm not. You aren't in Manhattan, Courtney. Finding a bear at your back door is no laughing matter."

"Tell me, Graham," Courtney said. "What's it going to be tomorrow? The big bad wolf? A giant comet plummeting through outer space headed straight for The Wooden Nickel? A tidal wave that's going to pick me up and wash me back to New York?"

"Cute."

Courtney didn't care. "I'm here for the summer. And nothing you come up with from bears at my back door to the bubonic plague is going to scare me into leaving."

Anger flickered in his dark brown eyes. "I wasn't trying to scare you. I was only stating the facts. And you being cavalier about the incinerator tells me I should have warned you about how important it is to dispose of your garbage every day."

Courtney sighed and said, "Look, I'm sorry if I sounded cavalier about the incinerator. I'll use it daily. Okay?"

"Okay," he said. "That's the answer I wanted."

Courtney could tell he wanted to say something else.

But Broadway barked. The bell on the front door came to life again.

And the Barlow twins strolled inside the store.

CHAPTER FOURTEEN

MARK BARLOW LET OUT a wolf whistle the second he saw Courtney. That caused Broadway to throw his head back in a bloodcurdling howl. But Graham's blood was curdling for a different reason.

He didn't like the leering grins on the twins' faces. He knew what they were thinking because he'd thought the same thing when she came downstairs.

Courtney had a body made for every man's fantasies.

"Ready, Courtney?" Clark asked, beaming.

Graham looked over at Courtney. "Ready for what?"

She glanced fondly at the twins. "Mark and Clark have invited me to go to Point Baker with them tonight while they play a little music."

"Dressed like *that?*" Graham boomed.

Courtney glanced innocently at her clothing, then back at the twins. "What about it, boys? Am I dressed okay for The Hitching Post?"

"Oh, yeah," they said in unison.

Their answer received a warning look from Graham.

Clark quickly looked away.

But Mark gulped and said, "Don't worry, Graham. We'll take good care of her."

"See?" Courtney said with a satisfied smile. "I

have my own personal bodyguards. I'll be perfectly safe."

She grabbed her fur-trimmed parka from the counter and sauntered to the door. It didn't surprise Graham when her so-called bodyguards scurried through the door ahead of her before Graham could get his hands on them.

Courtney stopped suddenly and turned back to face him.

"Oh, and Graham," she said sweetly, "since Rachel's already gone home, would you do me a big favor and lock up?" She smiled and patted her coat pocket. "And yes, I have my door key."

The door slammed shut behind her.

"Son of a bitch!"

Broadway whimpered at that comment.

"I've been worrying about the wrong kind of wildlife," Graham told the dog. "She'll see true wildlife when she gets to The Hitching Post. And dressed like that? She'll probably be mauled the second she walks through the door."

Broadway looked up at Graham, then back at the door. In fact, they both kept watching the door rather wistfully, as if they expected Courtney to rush back in at any minute to say she'd changed her mind.

She didn't.

"Fine," Graham said when he heard the familiar sound of a boat motor start up and roar away. "Let her go. It's nothing to me. If I'm lucky, she'll meet a guy she likes and get the hell out of *my* life."

Broadway whined in sympathy. But the dog's plaintive stare called Graham a liar.

"Don't look at me like that, you traitor," Graham warned. "You've already cost me a hundred bucks."

Broadway's ears instantly flattened against his head.

But the dog followed Graham's every step as he made the three trips it took to load his groceries into the skiff. When Graham made the last trip, Broadway entered the store, ready to take up his dutiful watch.

"See what you get for letting Rachel talk you into staying?" Graham scolded. "You'll be lucky if the woman you're supposed to be protecting makes it home by morning."

Broadway flopped down, his head resting on his paws.

"But if Rachel's right and you really do understand what I'm saying," Graham told the dog, "you have my permission to run those idiot twins out of here if they try any funny stuff later. Okay?"

Broadway sat back up and barked twice in agreement.

"Now, that's *my* idea of man's best friend," Graham told the dog as he flipped the door lock into place.

He walked to the dock, shaking his head in wonder at what Courtney was thinking, agreeing to go to some dive bar with the Barlow twins. Didn't she realize when a woman walked into a bar dressed the way she was, every guy there would automatically assume she was asking for it?

Graham suddenly stopped walking.

Maybe Courtney *was* asking for it. This time from a guy who would be willing to finish the job.

Graham cursed and stomped to the skiff.

As he sped away from The Wooden Nickel, there was one thing he did know for certain. It was going to be a long, hot summer for him despite Port Protection's usually mild weather.

Courtney's red-hot low-cut top.

Courtney's red-hot spike high heels.

And *his* red-hot reaction at the thought of someone else finishing what *he* hadn't been willing to do.

AS MUCH AS SHE LIKED the Barlow twins, Courtney had already decided this would be her only trip to hear them play their music. In the future, she would stay in Port Protection where she belonged.

She'd made a big mistake in coming. And now she was facing the consequences.

She'd kept her parka zipped all the way up to her eyebrows, but it hadn't changed a thing. There wasn't a man in the bar who hadn't already undressed her with his eyes at least once.

Courtney was thankful no one seemed to know what to do about her, except stare. Not one man had approached her yet. And as far as Courtney was concerned, that was fine by her.

But if the twins didn't finish their last set soon, she might be forced to start walking back to The Wooden Nickel. Even meeting up with a bear had to be better than this.

"Lover boy," the bartender called out when the door opened.

Out of curiosity, Courtney turned her head.

She found herself staring at the pilot who had brought her to Trail's End Lodge. Seconds later, Gil was sliding onto the stool beside her at the bar.

"What's a nice girl like you doing in a place like this?"

Courtney nodded toward her chaperones still playing music on the small stage in back of the bar. "The twins invited me. But I've been asking myself that same question from the moment we arrived."

Gil laughed and signaled to the bartender. "Bring me a cold one, Joe." He looked back at the bottle Courtney had sitting in front of her—the one she had barely touched all evening. "What about you? Ready for another?"

Courtney shook her head. "I don't think tipsy is a good thing to be in this crowd."

"Smart girl," Gil teased, grinning at her again.

He took a long sip from his beer before he cocked his head in her direction. "So? Would you like me to amuse you with my psychic abilities?"

"Sure. Why not?"

"You being here tells me two things." He held up the first finger. "One, Graham still has his head up his ass." He held up finger number two. "And two, you thought a night out with the Barlow twins might dislodge it for him. Right?"

"Close enough," Courtney admitted.

Gil shook his head. "I don't get it. Why do women always go for the strong, brooding, silent types like Graham?"

"As opposed to?" Courtney asked.

Gil held his arms out wide. "Guys like me who love everything about women."

"Did you ever stop to think earning a nickname like *lover boy* might be the reason women run the other way?"

"Trust me, darlin'," Gil said with a wink, "I've never had a problem with women running the other way." He grinned. "In fact, I think you're falling in love with me already."

He was too cocky for her liking. But Courtney could see why women didn't run the other way. Gil was tall, good-looking and blond. He had impossibly green eyes and perfect white teeth. Gil was the type of guy any woman would want in her bed—until she caught him in someone else's.

"So, tell me," Courtney said. "If you're so popular, what are you doing here all alone on a Friday night?"

"Point Baker's home for me. And I learned a valuable lesson a long time ago. Always keep your love life separate from your home base. When I'm home, I fly solo."

"How long have you been a pilot?"

"Now you're just fishing for my age."

"Then shall I amuse you with my physic abilities?"

"Absolutely," he said.

Courtney looked him up and down. "Fifty-what? Five?"

"Now that just plain hurt."

They both laughed.

But thanks to Gil, Courtney began to relax and enjoy herself. She forgot about the open stares and the curious glances still coming her way. Or the fact that she felt completely out of place being the only single woman in the bar. And as Gil shamelessly flirted with her, Courtney even forgot about Graham.

At least for a minute or two.

THE WOODEN NICKEL didn't open for business until nine in the morning—the reason Graham took immense satisfaction in pounding on the door at 6:00 a.m. Courtney had kept him from sleeping *at all* last night. It was only fair that he kept her from sleeping *in* this morning.

Broadway bounded through the door first and accepted Graham's greeting of a head rub before he darted off to do his morning business. That left Courtney standing in the doorway, one eye open, her hair a mess and wearing flannel pajamas and a pair of fuzzy bedroom slippers instead of the red high heels she'd been wearing the night before.

It didn't matter.

She was still the sexiest woman Graham had ever seen.

"Glad to see you're still alive."

She yawned. "And you couldn't have called to find that out?"

"You forgot my coffee," Graham said.

He walked past her and into the store. But instead of heading to the shelf for coffee, he walked across the store to the short-order grill. Whether Courtney wanted his advice or not, Graham was going to give it to her. The rules were different here. And running around to bars with the Barlow twins would send people the wrong message. She needed to know the score before her actions got her into big trouble.

Courtney climbed onto a stool at the counter, while Graham made coffee. "That was a stupid stunt you pulled going to The Hitching Post last night," he said, his back to her.

"I agree," she said. "Going was a mistake."

Graham turned around. It wasn't the response he'd been expecting from her. Had something bad happened?

"The twins didn't try anything with you, did they?"

She put her finger to her lips. "Shush. They're still sleeping. Threesomes are exhausting."

Graham immediately glanced toward the loft.

"I'm kidding," she said. "Of course the twins didn't try anything. If I even winked at the twins, they'd be climbing over each other trying to get out the door."

Had feeling foolish been a contest, Graham would have won first prize. "You shouldn't be so trusting. Not every man around here is as innocent as the Barlow twins."

She sighed. "What's your problem, Graham? We both know I didn't forget your coffee. Why are you here?"

"I feel responsible for you staying, okay?"

"Well, that's ridiculous. No one's responsible for me staying but me."

"And that line about me changing my mind?" Graham reminded her. "You don't see why that would make me feel responsible?"

She yawned again. Then she ran both hands over her beautiful face before she raked her fingers through her long, blond, wonderfully disheveled hair.

"You know what?" she said. "I'm really not awake enough to talk to you about this right now."

Graham turned to the coffeemaker, grabbed a cup from the counter and filled it with the steaming liquid. He placed the cup in front of her. "This should help wake you up."

She sighed. But she closed both hands around the mug and slowly brought it to her lips. After several sips, she looked up at him. "Okay, I have a question for you. Say I had gone back to New York. But before I got on the plane I told you that you knew where to find me in case you changed your mind. Would you feel responsible for me then?"

"Of course not," Graham said. "Your home is in New York."

"No," she said. "All I have in New York is an apartment. And I have a career that's been draining the lifeblood out of me for years. Do you know how long it's been since I've taken a vacation? The year I graduated from college when I spent three weeks touring Europe. Then I walked through the doors of Woods Advertising Agency and handed over my soul on a silver platter."

When Graham didn't say anything, she said, "I stayed for *me,* Graham. I need the time to figure out what I want to do with the rest of my life. So sorry if me staying is a problem for you. I'm not sure why it would be. You've made it clear you aren't interested."

Graham fixed a cup of coffee for himself. But he took his cup and walked around the counter and sat on the stool beside her. "I'd hoped I made it clear *why* I'm not interested. In anyone."

"That's something you have to work out for yourself," she said. "But I'm not sorry if my being here helps you come to the conclusion that you need to put the past behind you where it belongs. You're a better man than the one you were five years ago, Graham. Stop beating yourself up over the things you can't change and give yourself some credit for the changes you have made in your life."

She can see through your bullshit.

Graham quickly changed the subject.

"I'm sorry I woke you so early," he said. "I wanted to make sure you were okay. And I wanted to tell you to be careful while you're here, Courtney. You're a beautiful woman and you're going to attract a lot of attention."

She laughed. "You have to be blind to refer to me as beautiful. You've caught me looking like a mechanic, and now like some *hausfrau* in my flannel pajamas. *Beautiful* isn't exactly a word I would use to describe me."

"You can make light of what I'm saying," Graham said, "but some of the attention you attract might not be the kind you want. Just remember that."

"Thanks for the warning. I will."

She slid off the stool and padded around the counter to fill her cup again. When she turned back around, she said, "I have another question for you. How do you think people would react if I decided to host a community get-together every Friday night here at The Wooden Nickel?"

Graham answered with his first thought. "That could get expensive quick."

"Not if I kept the food simple. And if everyone brought or purchased what they wanted to drink here at the store."

"What made you think of that idea?"

"Something Gil said about The Hitching Post being the only place around here to go on a Friday night," she said. "And the fact that everyone had such a great time at your birthday party. I think it could liven things up."

Graham's grip had tightened on the handle of his cup the second Courtney said Gil's name. "Gil was at The Hitching Post last night?"

"He was nice enough to keep me company while the twins were onstage."

Nice my ass!

Nice wasn't the bone Gil had in his body where women were concerned. He was trouble. And if Graham hadn't already made himself look like such an idiot for grilling Courtney about the twins, he would tell her that.

"Gil's an expert on getting around. If he says there isn't anywhere else to go on Friday night, he's the one who would know."

"So you think it's a good idea to host something here?"

"I'm not the best person to ask about livening things up around here," Graham said, irritated that Courtney had missed his meaning completely. "I like things the way they are. I thought I'd made myself clear about that."

The minute he said it, Graham wished he hadn't. He hadn't meant to bark at her like that. But damn, this unexplained need he felt to protect Courtney—especially from guys like Gil—had overwhelmed him.

Now the damage was done.

And the look on her face said she was *wide*-awake now.

"OH, YOU'VE MADE yourself perfectly clear you like things the way they are," Courtney said, making sure her tone was as snippy as Graham had been with her. "But I wasn't thinking about livening things up for you. I was thinking about Rachel. I thought having something fun to do on Friday nights would make her happy."

"Making Rachel happy isn't your responsibility, Courtney."

"Maybe not. But I'm making it my responsibility while I'm here."

She hadn't intended to have this conversation with Graham. Not now. Maybe not ever. But his condescending, overbearing and plain damn irritating attitude had pushed her where she hadn't planned to go.

"Teenage depression can be serious, Graham. I found that out the hard way when I was Rachel's age. I lost a close friend because everyone, including me, didn't realize how depressed she was."

"What are you implying, Courtney? That you think Rachel would hurt herself?"

"No. I don't *think* she would. But she made that threat and it wasn't a chance I was willing to take. That's another reason I decided to stay. As much as Rachel loves you, there are things a teenage girl can't talk to her father about. I hoped if we had the summer together, maybe I could—"

"I've heard enough," he said, sliding off the stool.

He dug a five dollar bill out of his pocket and tossed it onto the counter. "Thanks for the coffee," he said. "And for pointing out that I'm still such a lousy father my daughter is threatening suicide."

"You know you aren't a lousy father," Courtney said, hurrying after him as Graham headed for the door.

He whirled around to face her. Courtney stopped short when Graham pointed a finger at her.

"You should have told me the minute Rachel made such a threat."

"Do you want to know why I didn't tell you? I couldn't bring myself to dump that information on you only hours after you'd told me how guilty you felt about Julia. I knew you would do exactly what you're doing now. You'd make Rachel's depression about you instead of facing the real issue."

"And you don't think my daughter threatening to harm herself is the real issue?" he shouted.

"No!" Courtney yelled back. "The real issue is that Rachel is going through a phase where she isn't happy here, Graham. And instead of flexing your father muscles and telling her too bad that you're the boss and there's nothing she can do about it, you might want to start thinking about ways to make Rachel happy living here."

"Isn't it amazing that it's always the people who don't have children who claim to know what's best for them?"

If he'd meant to hurt her, his comment worked.

Courtney didn't try to stop him when Graham slammed out of the store. And though she wanted to call Rachel and at least warn her about their discussion, Courtney didn't.

Graham was right. She should have told him she was concerned about Rachel immediately. Rachel was his child, not hers. And now that the issue was out into the open, she had to back off and let Graham handle it.

But Courtney's gut told her Graham wouldn't do anything stupid. Even though Graham was furious with her for not telling him, he was still an excellent father. He was also smart enough to know the worst thing he could do under the circumstances was make Rachel quit her job at the store and break all contact with the one person she trusted enough to tell what was on her mind.

If anything, this discussion strengthened Courtney's resolve to liven things up by playing hostess on Friday nights. The Barlow twins had already agreed to forgo their gig at The Hitching Post in favor of her hiring them to play at The Wooden Nickel. Unless she got a flat thumbs-down from the rest of the community, people in Port Protection were going to have a weekly social.

She wanted to give something back to the community that had been gracious enough to accept her. And she wasn't going to worry about the expense of these events. She'd pay out of her own pocket. And so what if Graham probably wouldn't participate after the big blowup they'd had.

Rachel would be thrilled.

Broadway barked and Courtney opened the door to let him in. She caught the last glimpse of Graham's skiff disappearing around the cove.

The big dummy.

She hadn't been trying to make him feel responsible for her staying when she'd told him he knew where to find her. She'd only been trying to point out that she was interested in him, not his past.

She'd arrived on the thirtieth of May, the day before Graham's birthday. And though she'd never put much stock in astrology, being born under the zodiac sign of the Gemini twins fit Graham to a T. He seemed to be constantly trying to reconcile the two opposite sides of his dual personality.

But she was Aquarian—the water bearer—concerned for the welfare of all. Her concern for all of their futures was why Courtney wouldn't give up even though today was already the last day of June, and Graham had discouraged her so much a weaker woman would have buckled.

Courtney had two months left and she intended to make the most of them.

CHAPTER FIFTEEN

BY THE TIME GRAHAM reached the lodge, his anger at Courtney had subsided. He could understand why a tragedy in her past would make Courtney take Rachel's threat seriously. But his daughter's dramatics were wearing thin and fast.

This time, Rachel had gone too far. And Graham intended to call her on it.

But he wouldn't throw Courtney under the bus. At least, not completely. He owed her that much for being honest with him.

Graham found Rachel at the dining room table, a bowl of her *stale* cereal in front of her. She sent him a sleepy look when he walked through the door.

"Where have you been?"

"I just had an interesting conversation with Courtney."

Rachel looked pleased until Graham said, "Courtney's concerned about your depression. Any idea why she would feel that way?"

He'd expected to see a little shame in her eyes.

When he didn't, Graham made his decision.

"When you get through with your cereal, Rachel, I want you to spend the rest of the day packing. You're leaving for New York on Monday."

She gasped. "But, Dad. I can't go to New York. Not now. Courtney stayed here for the summer because of me."

"Why do you care?" Graham demanded. "You invited Courtney as a way to get to New York. You scared her into staying, hoping she would still be your ticket out of here. You've proved you're willing to do anything and say anything to get what you want. So you win, Rachel. And as soon as I make your plane reservations, I'm calling my parents to tell them when to pick you up at the airport."

Graham walked across the great room and into his office. By the time he sat down at his computer and started an airline search, Rachel was rushing through his office door.

"Please don't do this, Dad," she begged. "I didn't mean to scare Courtney. All I said was that the thought of spending another summer here with nothing to do made me want to kill myself, and she freaked. But I wasn't serious, Dad. I swear it."

"I'm not willing to take that chance," Graham said. "So stop making excuses and start packing."

Graham didn't even look at her. He kept his eyes focused on the screen as the Web site for airline reservations popped up. He typed in the information and hit the submit button.

"Dammit, Dad! You aren't listening to me."

"*You* watch your language."

Her voice trembled when she said, "Don't you realize I never wanted to live with my grandparents? That I was only trying to get *you* to move there? And yes, I did invite Courtney hoping she might give you a reason to return, since you wouldn't do it for me. But the only way I want to live in New York is if you go with me, Dad. And if you aren't going with me I'm not going, either."

Graham finally faced her. "Give up this opportunity now and you won't get another one," he warned. "You'll be stuck in this *miserable* place until you go to college."

Rachel didn't answer.

"And if it's Courtney you're still worried about, she'll be back in New York by the end of the summer. Then you'll have everything you want."

"Except you," Rachel said, her lower lip trembling.

"My home is here, Rachel. And so is my business. We've had this same discussion a million times. So make your decision. Either go back to New York now, or stay here. I'm tired of arguing about it."

"But couldn't we compromise, Dad?" she pleaded. "I'm willing to if you are. We could live here in the summer, since that's your peak season. But we could live in New York during the school year so I could go to a regular high school. And you'd only have to do that for the next three years, Dad. Then I would go to college, and you could live here full-time again."

Graham kept staring at her.

Never once had Rachel mentioned a compromise in the past. Their arguments had always been about moving to New York permanently. But it only took a nanosecond for Graham to realize where Rachel got the idea.

"Let me guess," he said. "Compromising was Courtney's solution."

"Yes," Rachel said. "And when I told her you'd never consider it, Courtney told me I'd never know unless I asked. So now I've asked."

Before Graham could comment, Rachel said, "But it's obvious Courtney was wrong about you listening to me if I opened up and told you how I really feel about things. You haven't heard a word I said. You'd rather be mad because it was Courtney's idea."

Rachel kicked his ass with that comment.

Because it was true.

His first reaction was to be pissed. "Did I say I wouldn't consider a compromise?" Graham asked, trying to save face.

Rachel blinked. "You mean you'll think about us living in New York for the school year?"

"New York, no," Graham said. "Ketchikan or Anchorage, maybe."

Rachel's face fell.

"Both of those places have large high schools you could attend, Rachel. And we'd be close enough to fly home on weekends so I could look after things here. That's the compromise I'm willing to think about. Take it, or leave it."

"Whatever," Rachel said, and walked out of his office.

Graham sighed. There were times when he had no choice but to flex his father muscles as Courtney had accused, and this was one of them. But he also kept thinking about Courtney's claim that he was a better man than the one he'd been five years ago.

Maybe he was.

Five years ago he wouldn't have considered a compromise. Hell, he wouldn't have considered a compromise five weeks ago.

However, five weeks ago he wasn't aware that his daughter was so desperate to go to a regular high school she was masquerading as him on the Internet. That alone had been a wake-up call. And the scare Rachel had given Courtney only confirmed that, at least for the next three years, he was going to have to make some changes.

Change.

His grandfather always said the only consistent thing in life was change. A more true statement, Graham couldn't imagine.

A change had been going on inside him from the moment Courtney arrived. And Graham wasn't sure if he should curse Courtney for it, or thank her for it.

Courtney had definitely gotten under his skin.

Just as Frank had crooned.

HAD IT NOT BEEN FOR HER frequent morning chats with Beth, Courtney's contact with the outside world would have been nonexistent. Life went on in Port Protection as if it were a tiny planet of its own. And if anyone in Port Protection other than Rachel was concerned that life might be passing them by, no one let on.

That's why Courtney had Beth on the phone now.

"So? What do you think?"

Beth groaned. "I think you should abandon your Friday night social club and come home where you belong."

Courtney laughed. "Make fun of me if you want. But you just gave me a great slogan for my marketing campaign: Welcome to the Friday Night Social Club. Your home away from home."

"And when you're standing in the unemployment line this fall, I'll remind you of the marketing campaigns you should have been working on instead of playing social director for some hick town in Alaska."

"Good try," Courtney said, "but I'm ignoring your bitchy remark. And since you aren't giving me the support I need, now I'm hanging up."

Courtney did just that. And she didn't give a second thought about it. That was one of the benefits of having a best friend. If you didn't like what she was saying, you could hang up knowing you'd still be best friends when you called back later.

Courtney replaced the receiver on the wall phone hanger as the bell sounded above the door. When she turned around, Graham's best friend walked into the store.

"Good morning," Courtney called out.

Yanoo mumbled the same greeting in her direction as he headed for the section Hal had devoted to hardware, plumbing and hunting supplies. Courtney was waiting for Yanoo at the cash register when he placed a paintbrush and a can of something called Ready Seal on the counter in front of her.

She'd sat at this man's table, and he was a regular customer in the store. Yet, he'd hardly said more than a few words to her. It was obvious he didn't think much of her. Courtney didn't care. Today she was going to force Yanoo to talk to her whether he liked it or not.

Courtney handed over his change before she said, "Can I ask you a question?"

Yanoo looked apprehensive at that request.

Courtney said, "Next week is the Fourth of July and I was thinking about hosting a party for the community on Friday night. Do you think people would come?"

"Yes."

"Do you think people would come if I hosted a party every Friday night for the rest of the summer?"

"Yes."

Frustrated, Courtney said, "You don't like me very much, do you, Yanoo? You think I'm some crazy woman from New York trying to get her hooks into your best friend."

His expression remained passive when he said, "Are you some crazy woman from New York trying to get her hooks into my best friend?"

"Yes, I'm crazy. I'm crazy about Graham. But the feeling isn't mutual, so you don't have anything to worry about."

Yanoo picked up the can and the paintbrush before he looked at her and said, "Graham is complicated, but he's a good man. Don't give up on him too soon. And if I didn't like you, I wouldn't give you that advice."

Yanoo didn't wait for a reply. He left Courtney standing at the counter, completely shocked.

But she didn't get the chance to analyze what Yanoo had said. The minute Yanoo walked out of the store, Rachel stormed through the front door.

Courtney braced herself.

"Thanks a lot for telling Dad why you stayed," she said, her lips in a surly pout as she stalked in Courtney's direction.

"I should have told him earlier, Rachel. And I'm not going to apologize for telling him now."

Rachel boosted herself up onto the counter and sat with her arms crossed. "Well, thanks to you, Dad threatened to send me to New York to live with my grandparents."

"I'm confused. I thought that's what you wanted."

"I never wanted to live with my grandparents. I want

to live in New York, sure. But I don't want to live there without Dad."

Courtney smiled inwardly. The parent-child bond was an amazing thing.

But Courtney's heart sank a little at that thought. She hadn't heard from her mother since the morning she'd announced she was staying. Of course, she also hadn't called her mother.

But she would.

At some point.

When Courtney knew what she did want for her future.

Rachel looked over at her. "Having that big talk you suggested about a compromise didn't work, either. Dad's idea of a compromise is us living in Ketchikan or Anchorage during the school year. He said we'd be close enough to fly home on weekends so he could check on things here."

"But, Rachel, that's wonderful. Think about it. I'm sure you can find a great high school in either of those cities."

"Dad only said he'd *think* about it," Rachel grumbled. "He has the rest of the summer to change his mind."

He has the rest of the summer to change his mind.

Courtney pushed the significance of those words aside. "Speaking of the rest of the summer, I've decided I'm going to start hosting a party here at The Wooden Nickel on Friday nights and invite everyone in town. What do you think about that idea?"

Rachel hopped down from the counter. "Are you kidding? That would be awesome."

"Then we have a lot of planning to do. Think we could get Tiki and Hanya to help us?"

Rachel immediately ran for the wall phone. While she

talked to Tiki, Courtney's thoughts went back to what Yanoo said about not giving up on Graham too soon.

It was the glimmer of hope she'd been looking for. If anyone knew Graham, it was Yanoo.

And that's when she remembered the rescue squad meeting Graham and Yanoo would be attending tonight. That meant Graham would be at the town hall center only a few buildings away from the store. It also meant he would leave his skiff at the dock below the store that everyone used when they came into town.

She could wait and see if Graham would stop by the store on his own, which was highly doubtful. Or she could watch for him after the meeting and make the first move toward getting past the argument.

The decision should have been easy.

But it wasn't.

Yanoo describing Graham as complicated was an understatement. Maybe she should give him time to cool down before she tried to approach him. But every day that passed was one day closer to the end of her stay.

"Tiki and Hanya would love to help," Rachel called out when she hung up the phone. "They're going to stop by after we close the store. And since our guests are finally gone at the lodge, Tiki wants me to spend the night with her. That means we'll have all night to plan the party."

"Great." It was the only thing Courtney *could* say. The decision about Graham had been made for her.

CHAPTER SIXTEEN

AFTER THE MEETING, Graham stayed to talk with the group of guys who always hung around to swap a few lies before they went home. It was something Graham usually didn't do. But Rachel wasn't home alone waiting for him tonight.

She'd called earlier, excited about the party Courtney was planning and begging to spend the night with Tiki since their lodge guests were gone.

Rachel had earned some time off.

She'd surprised him. She'd kept up with all of her chores despite the fact that she'd worked at the store for Courtney every day.

Graham was proud of her.

Maybe that's why he'd been so knocked over when Courtney told him what Rachel had threatened. Rachel's emotions had been all over the place for over a year now. Up one day. Down the next.

It made Graham crazy.

Even Rachel didn't know what she wanted. She'd proved that this morning when she'd refused to go to New York when he'd finally had enough and offered to send her to live with his parents.

He should have called Rachel's bluff the first time she

mentioned going back to New York. If he had, maybe the Courtney situation wouldn't have happened. And he wouldn't be standing here now, pretending to follow the conversation and pretending that he didn't care Courtney was in close proximity only a few buildings away.

"What about you, Graham?"

Graham looked up to find one of his fellow fisherman staring at him. "Sorry, Bill. I missed the question."

"Are you booked up for the Fourth?"

"Yeah," Graham said. "My guests are arriving on Wednesday."

"Same here," Bill said. "It's going to be a busy week."

"I hear there's going to be a big party at The Wooden Nickel Friday night," one of the guys said. "Whole town's invited."

Graham didn't comment on that subject. And not because he opposed Courtney's party. He'd be tied up with his guests all weekend.

"Is anyone going to enter the Woodsman contest this year?" Bill asked, looking over at Graham again.

Graham laughed. "Don't look at me."

The contest was a local charity fundraiser with the typical events—wood splitting, ax-throwing and pole climbing. The final event was what people really paid to see. The freestyle wrestling match that decided the winner provided enough blood and guts to give people their money's worth.

Bill said, "I hope someone takes Gil Hargraves's title away from him this year. The bastard. I've been waiting to see someone kick his ass for four years."

Graham could sympathize with the way Bill felt about Gil. Gil had once dated Bill's daughter, and as usual, Gil hadn't kept many of the details to himself. Someone was going to shut Gil's mouth for him one day. And like Bill, Graham hoped he was around to see it happen.

He'd already decided he was going to have a talk with Gil on Wednesday when he brought Graham's guests to the lodge. He intended to tell Gil that Courtney was off-limits before Courtney found herself in a situation she couldn't handle.

The group started breaking up and Graham headed for the door with everyone else, but Yanoo signaled for him to wait a minute. Yanoo walked to the far side of the meeting room and picked up a paper sack sitting on a table in the corner. When he returned, he handed the sack to Graham.

Graham looked at him, puzzled. "What's this for?"

"Incentive," Yanoo said. "That's an expensive bottle of wine and the moon's full tonight. Don't waste it."

"Don't *you* push it," Graham warned, following Yanoo to the door.

"I have to pick up Hanya and Tiki at the store, so I can take Rachel, too," Yanoo said as they walked through the center of town.

"Thanks," Graham said. "That means I can get home even sooner than I expected."

When Yanoo stopped at the store, Graham kept walking. He'd call and say good-night to Rachel later. Two minutes more and he was pulling away from the dock below the store.

To hell with Yanoo and his wine and the damn full moon.

Graham was going home.

WHEN GRAHAM DIDN'T stop at the store with Yanoo, Courtney was thankful she hadn't had the opportunity to make a fool of herself by waylaying Graham after his meeting. Evidently, he was still too angry to talk to her. With the way her luck had been running, he'd stay angry with her for the remainder of the summer.

But she wasn't going to worry about it tonight. It wasn't worth losing sleep over.

She finished putting away the last of the food. She wiped the lunch counter down. And she had just turned out the light above the grill when Broadway whined and trotted to the door.

"You just went out when Rachel left, silly," Courtney told him, but she headed to the door anyway.

When she opened it, Graham was standing there.

He held up a bottle of wine. "This is a great Merlot. There's an amazing full moon tonight. And all I need are two wineglasses, a corkscrew and someone willing to sit outside and enjoy it with a guy who's sorry for being such a jerk this morning."

"Tonight's your lucky night," Courtney told him. "You came to the right place."

She grabbed the glasses and the corkscrew. The full moon had little to do with Graham's preference to sit outside. He was offering a truce, but he still intended to keep his distance from her. Courtney would take that.

It was better than not seeing Graham at all.

She found him sitting on the top step of the landing leading down to the dock, Broadway stretched out behind him. Courtney stepped over Broadway and sat beside Graham. When she handed over the corkscrew, he opened the bottle, filled both glasses and placed the bottle on the step between them.

They sat in silence, sipping wine and watching the moonlight dance across the water. Courtney decided to let Graham take the lead when it came to the conversation. He'd shown up on her doorstep to apologize. But Courtney could tell Graham had more than wine and moonlight on his mind tonight.

They sat in silence a little longer.

He finally looked over at her. "What were you like in high school?"

Courtney laughed out of sheer relief. She'd been so sure Graham intended to ask her to go home again.

"What made you think of that?"

"Rachel," he said. "I've been thinking about my high school years. All the memories. They were some of the best times of my life. So thanks for encouraging Rachel to talk to me about a compromise, even if she isn't thrilled about Anchorage or Ketchikan. Rachel needs the opportunity to have good high school memories of her own. I was being selfish not to realize that."

"You and Rachel would have eventually reached the same conclusion without my help," Courtney said.

"I don't think so," he said. "Our problem has been not talking. Until you came, all we were doing was yelling at each other. So thank you for that, too. You've acted as the buffer we needed between us to make us look at the situation from the other person's point of view."

"Thanks for saying that, Graham. I'm glad I've been able to help."

He refilled his glass and leaned over to refill hers. Their shoulders only touched for a second. But it was long enough to make Courtney gulp down half her glass. She had to get her mind off how close they were sitting before she took him by the hand and led him straight to bed.

"Let me guess what you were like in high school. Total football jock, of course. Cheerleader girlfriend. Most popular guy. Prom king." She grinned at him. "Close?"

"Embarrassing, but yes," he said. "Now it's my turn. Homecoming queen. *Captain* of the football team for a boyfriend. Most beautiful. Prom *queen.* How am I doing so far?"

"Batting zero," Courtney said. "I was beanpole thin in high school, two inches taller than any guy in school and I had braces until my second year in college. I was a total geekette. Chess club president. Captain of the debate club. Editor of the school newspaper *and* the yearbook."

"No wonder you always kick my butt every time we have an argument."

He was only teasing and Courtney knew it.

But it gave her the opportunity to say, "About that. I like it much better when we don't argue, Graham. Like now, just sitting here talking. It's nice. Don't you think?"

GRAHAM ALMOST MISSED the question. She was leaning forward with her elbows on her knees, her long hair over one shoulder, staring at him with eyes so blue he could see the depth of the color in the moonlight. One more second and he'd have her in his arms.

He couldn't do that to her again.

He *wouldn't* do that to her again.

He shouldn't even be here now. He'd been almost at the lodge when he'd turned the skiff around, knowing if he didn't clear the air with Courtney, he wouldn't sleep at all.

But sitting in the moonlight together had been a bad idea. Looking at her made him want her so bad right now Graham ached all over. But the key words were *right now.*

Courtney deserved forever.

Graham wasn't sure he'd ever have forever to give.

He picked up the wine bottle between them, glad to see there was only enough left to add a splash in each glass.

"This has been nice," Graham said, finally answering her question. He polished off his wine and stood. "We'll have to do it again sometime."

She stood, as well. "I hope you'll come to the party Friday night."

"Sorry," Graham told her, "but I'll have a lodge full of guests starting on Wednesday. And when men pay to come here, believe me, all they want to do is fish."

He started down the steps.

"Thanks for the wine," she called out.

Graham stopped walking and turned around. "I can't come to your party, but I could make coffee for you again in the morning before I pick Rachel up at Yanoo's. Are you up for that?"

"At six o'clock?" She shook her head. "Thanks, but I'll pass."

"How about seven?"

"Make it eight and we have a deal."

"Eight it is."

"Good night, Graham."

Graham threw his hand up in a wave as he headed to the skiff.

But he did glance over his shoulder as he pulled away

from the dock. He could see her silhouette in the moonlight, still standing on the landing, Broadway beside her.

She waved.

For a second, Graham felt a little less empty inside.

COURTNEY FELT SILLY lying in bed in the dark grinning from ear to ear. But she couldn't help it. Maybe Graham had only stopped by to apologize. She'd even detected the exact minute he got nervous and decided to leave—she'd seen the desire in his eyes before he got his emotions under control.

It didn't matter.

Graham was coming back for coffee in the morning.

That meant, whether he realized it or not, she was slowly breaking through some of that stone wall he'd built around himself for protection. And that told Courtney she'd done the right thing by hanging back and letting Graham come to her.

Is that what Yanoo meant by not giving up too soon?

Courtney could only wonder.

She'd told Yanoo she was crazy about Graham. But her feelings went much deeper than that. She'd been infatuated with Graham—or at least the idea of Graham—before she arrived in Port Protection. But she'd fallen in love with Graham that day at the gazebo.

She loved him.

Graham could learn to love her back.

Or Graham could decide to let her go.

But Courtney would love him still.

ON WEDNESDAY, GRAHAM sent his guests up to the lodge to help themselves to the refreshments he had waiting for them and stayed to help Gil unload the luggage. He intended to use the opportunity to have a little conversation about Courtney.

Gil beat Graham to it.

"Just to put you on notice," Gil said, "I'm asking Courtney out at her party Friday night."

"I don't think so."

"What's the problem?" Gil jeered. "You aren't interested in her. If you were, she'd be in your bed instead of minding the general store."

"It doesn't matter," Graham said. "Courtney's off-limits."

"Well, I guess we'll leave that up to Courtney to decide, won't we? And we both know who has the best track record when it comes to being persuasive with women."

"Do the smart thing and back off, Gil."

Gil's smirk vanished. "Is that a threat, Graham?"

"If you have to ask that question," Graham said, "you haven't been listening."

For a second Graham thought Gil was going to hit him.

Instead, Gil walked past him and climbed into the cockpit of the plane. Graham stayed where he was, staring directly at Gil, but Gil refused to make eye contact.

Graham was still standing on the dock when the floatplane disappeared around the cove. He hoped Gil would take him at his word and make the wise decision to leave Courtney alone.

Courtney going out with Gil wasn't the problem.

The problem was Courtney turning Gil down.

If she did turn Gil down—and Graham had enough faith in Courtney to think that she would—Gil wouldn't be happy about it and things could turn ugly quick. And that's when Graham would have to step in and back up his threat.

He hadn't kept Julia safe when he should have.

He wouldn't make that same mistake with Courtney.

CHAPTER SEVENTEEN

"CAN I ASK you something?"

Courtney looked up from her sweeping to Rachel, who was wiping the counter at the grill. The usual lunch crew had finally left, their busiest part of the day was over, and now they were alone in the store.

"You know you can ask me anything, sweetie," Courtney said, smiling at her.

"Are you in love with my dad?"

Hmm, except maybe that. "Why?"

"Still hoping, I guess," Rachel said with a sigh. "And Dad does have coffee with you when we don't have guests. I was hoping that meant you both had finally figured out that you're perfect for each other."

Rachel went back to wiping the counter.

Courtney continued sweeping.

Graham had been stopping by for coffee whenever he could, and though Courtney looked forward to those small slices of time she had with him, he hadn't offered her anything more. Nor had he shown up at the Friday night gatherings, even though they were a huge success.

It was the middle of July, and time was running out fast. Each day that passed led Courtney steadily toward accepting the fact that Graham never would change his mind about letting himself love anyone again.

That meant she had to get serious about what she wanted to do. Her wish-list future would be marrying the man she loved and becoming an official mother to Rachel. She loved them both. And she wouldn't care if they lived in Port Protection, or Ketchikan, or Anchorage or Timbuktu.

Home was where the heart is. And Graham and Rachel had stolen her heart completely.

Courtney glanced at Rachel again.

She was so proud of Rachel, and she told Rachel that on a daily basis. Rachel was quick and assertive and didn't have to be told what to do before she took the initiative to do it. Courtney had made it a point to work Rachel's butt off, yet never once had Rachel complained.

But today something was bothering Rachel. Deciding to find out what that something was, Courtney propped her broom against the counter and slid onto the stool in front of Rachel.

"Let's take a break," Courtney said. "And you can tell me what's going on inside that pretty head of yours."

Rachel walked around the counter to plop on the stool beside Courtney. "What makes you think something's going on?"

"You seem a little down today."

Rachel said, "Did you get the invitation to Peg and Hal's anniversary party?"

"I did," Courtney said. "The invitations are beautiful, aren't they?"

"Are you going?"

"Yes."

"Lucky you," Rachel mumbled.

Courtney didn't dare bring up the fact that since the party was being held on Labor Day weekend in Seattle, and Peg and Hal would be coming home on Labor Day Monday, she would return to New York from Seattle, not from Port Protection. "I guess that means Graham is refusing to go?"

"How incredibly brilliant of you."

"And that's what has you feeling down today?"

"That and a zillion other things."

"Such as?"

Rachel looked over at her. "Have you ever heard of a wish basket?"

Courtney shook her head. "No. I can't say that I have."

"Tiki has one," Rachel said. "Every Haida girl has one. I've seen baskets like hers at the craft shop Tiki's aunt opens for the tourists. I just didn't know what they were."

"You mean the large trunklike baskets with the lids?"

Rachel nodded. "Except Tiki's aunt didn't make her basket. Tiki's grandmother made it after she was born. Tiki and her mom have been putting things in it for when she gets married."

"Oh," Courtney said. "That's the same thing we call a hope chest. I don't think many people keep that tradition anymore, but people once used cedar chests for girls to store their prenuptial things."

"Do you have a hope chest?"

Courtney shook her head.

"Me, either," Rachel said. "And it really made me jealous when I saw Tiki's. She and her mom have made all kinds of things. Little hand towels with fancy embroidery. And Haida bracelets and hair combs for Tiki's wedding ceremony. She and her mom made them from shells they've collected along the beaches around here. Tiki even has her mom's wedding outfit in her wish basket. She'll wear the same clothes when she gets married that her mom wore the day Tiki's parents were married."

Courtney sighed. "Well, if it makes you feel any better, now I'm jealous, too."

"Really?"

"Really. But you know that gives me an idea. Why don't we start our own wish baskets?"

Rachel sat up straight. "Are you serious?"

"Why not? We'll go pick out our wish baskets tomorrow. Maybe we could even ask Tiki and Hanya if they would show us how to make bracelets and combs."

"Awesome," Rachel said, beaming.

"You might want to ask your grandmothers if they have anything personal and homemade they want to contribute."

Rachel laughed. "You haven't met my grandmothers. I love them both, but if it doesn't have a designer label, it doesn't exist for either of them."

"Did you ever consider that might be one of the reasons your dad wanted to raise you here in Alaska? So you would realize there were more important things in life than designer labels?"

"Did my dad tell you that?"

"Yeah, he did."

She'd had that conversation with Graham the last time he had dropped by for coffee, which had been three days, seven hours and about fifteen minutes ago. But who was counting?

"Dad and I never talk about stuff like that."

"Maybe you should." Courtney gave Rachel a nudge with her elbow.

"I don't see that happening."

"Give him a chance, Rachel. Ask him point-blank why he feels the way he does about things. And instead of getting angry if you don't like his answer, don't be afraid to tell him how you feel about things, too. He doesn't have to like your reasons any more than you like his. The important thing is that you talk to each other instead of holding everything in. The more you hold stuff in, the more it hurts. And the more it hurts, the more miserable you become."

"What am I going to do without you when you go back to New York?"

Courtney put on a brave smile. "You can talk to me every day if you need to, just like you're doing now. And we've already established ourselves as the e-mail queens of the Internet."

"It won't be the same as having you here."

"No," Courtney agreed, "it won't be the same as me living within walking distance. But no matter where I live, or where you live, Rachel, I'll always be there for you. You can count on that. Always."

Rachel leaned over and hugged her. "I love you, Courtney."

Courtney blinked back tears. "I love you, too, Rachel."

COURTNEY SENT RACHEL home early that afternoon for two reasons. Wednesdays were always slow. And in the process of trying to cheer Rachel up, she'd actually brought herself down. This definitely called for a chat with Beth.

"Are you crying?"

"No," Courtney lied and blew her nose.

"That's a sound effect I could have done without," Beth fussed. "Spit it out, Courtney. What the bloody hell is going on?"

"Bloody hell?" Courtney repeated. "You've never used that expression in your life."

"Deal with it," Beth said. "I'm dating a Brit at the moment."

"Since when?"

"Since last night around midnight when I met him at that new martini bar I told you about," Beth said. "He's picking me up at seven. So that gives you thirty minutes to tell me what's wrong."

"Please tell me you didn't sleep with him."

"Okay. I won't tell you."

"Beth!"

"Oh, no, you don't. You are not going to call me when it's obvious you've been crying, and then try to change the subject and give me a lecture."

"I'm just having a bad day, okay? And I hate to admit it, but everything you warned me about is coming true. You told me it was a big mistake trying to play the mother role to Rachel. And you warned me I was being a fool to think Graham would change his mind. Summer's almost over, Beth. So you tell me? What in the bloody hell am I going to do when I can't bear the thought of Graham and Rachel not being in my life?"

"I'll tell you what you're going to do. You're going to come back to reality and leave this fantasy all-I-want-is-a-family world you've been living in behind you. Seriously, Courtney. I don't care if you do love Graham.

You've been sitting there for almost two months and the most he's willing to offer you is stopping by for a cup of coffee now and then. And don't get me started on the situation with Rachel. I might understand if Rachel was an infant who desperately needed a mother's love and care. But the girl is practically grown."

Courtney sniffed. "Well, I disagree. I think you need a mother's love and care no matter how old you are."

"Bingo!" Beth exclaimed. "And there, in a nutshell, lies the root of your problem. You're trying to act out with Rachel the type of relationship you've always wanted with your mother."

"Thank you, Dr. Phil."

"Whatever. Lie to yourself if it makes you feel better. But we both know what I said is true."

All she'd wanted was a little sympathy from Beth. What she'd gotten was a reminder of what a big fat liar she was. She'd given such great advice to Rachel, telling her she needed to talk to her father instead of holding it all in. Pointing out that the longer you held things in, the more it hurt and the worse it became.

Liar.

She was a big fat liar!

And it had taken Beth to call her on it.

"I wasn't going to tell you this," Beth said, "but Lisa has been calling me at least once a week to check on you."

Okay. That was startling. "And?"

"Only because I love you," Beth said, "I've been giving Lisa the rose-colored glasses version of your little vacation. How the peace and solitude has been extremely cathartic for you. How you've gotten completely in touch with your inner self. In other words, enough new age bullshit that Lisa can save face when people ask about you. I'm sure, with her spin, everyone will find your summer seclusion amazingly chic."

"You do know Mother so well."

"True," Beth said. "In fact, I've been so convincing maybe Lisa will take the whole sainted team to Alaska next summer to share the same experience and then, lucky you will have another opportunity to drop in on Graham."

Sainted team.

It was the tag Beth had given the department heads at the agency—the team her mother kept glued to her side, even to the point she demanded everyone's presence for Sunday brunch, no exceptions.

"You're forgetting. I'm not part of the sainted team anymore."

"Oh, please. Lisa isn't going to fill your position, Courtney. And you're lying if you say you really thought she would."

"Did Mother ask you to tell me that?" Her mother could save face and still get what she wanted—Courtney back in the fold.

"No. But the fact Lisa made it a point to tell me she wasn't replacing you was the same thing as asking me to tell you."

"Well, whether you believe me or not, living here *has* been cathartic for me. I'm not the same person. And a lot of things would have to change before I would ever agree to work for my mother again. A forty-hour work week for starters. Period. No exceptions. And weekends off. And no more excruciating Sunday brunches. And scheduled vacations. And—"

"Why are you telling me this?" Beth asked flatly.

"Good question," Courtney said and hung up.

It took Courtney another hour before she was ready to call her mother. And thanks to Beth for letting her vent, by the time she was ready to make the call all of Courtney's anger was gone.

She loved her mother and she missed her.

And Courtney intended to tell her that.

Her mother answered her cell on the first ring.

"Mom. It's me."

There was a long pause before her mother said, "You haven't called me *Mom* since you were a child."

"Maybe it's because I've been acting like a child and I'm so sorry it's taken this long for me to figure that out. I love you, Mom. And I miss you. And I didn't stay in Alaska to hurt you. I had reached a crossroads in my life where I wanted something more than a career. But instead of telling you that like an adult, I guess I ran away from home." There. She'd said it. And doing so wasn't nearly as hard as she'd expected.

"And do you love this man?"

"Yes," Courtney said without hesitation.

"And are you sure he loves you?"

"No," Courtney said. "That's why I stayed, Mom. I needed to find out."

CHAPTER EIGHTEEN

FRIDAY NIGHTS AT The Wooden Nickel were always fun for Courtney. But on this particular Friday night having a fun time wasn't the only reason for the smile on Courtney's face.

It was the end of July now. But finally—*finally*—Graham had shown up.

He was at the pool table with Yanoo now.

The very sight of him took her breath away.

Courtney turned back to the oven, humming along with the country tune the Barlow twins were playing, and peeking through the glass oven door at the pizza she promised Rachel and Tiki she would keep an eye on. The timer buzzed so Courtney turned off the oven. She intended to remind the girls she deserved at least a tiny slice of their pizza for making sure it didn't burn.

She had just reached for a mitt to remove the pizza when the guy who had made it a point to show up every Friday night—the last guy she wanted to see—walked through the door with a cooler in his hand. She'd told Gil from the time he asked her out she wasn't interested. But his smiling face kept showing up every Friday night hoping he would eventually catch her at a weak moment and she'd finally give in.

It wasn't going to happen.

She'd even been outright rude to Gil last week so it irked her that he was here tonight. Especially since Graham was here.

She'd wanted to have the entire night to focus on Graham and only Graham. But the leer on Gil's face as he walked in her direction told Courtney she'd be fighting him off all evening.

"Hello, beautiful," Gil said, grinning at her.

"You need a new line," Courtney said. "That one's getting old."

Gil glanced past her at the pool table. "But, darlin', I thought *old* turned you on."

It wasn't the first time he'd made a snide comment about Graham, but Courtney had always ignored him. Just as she was ignoring him now. Gil's game was getting a rise out of someone. Courtney wouldn't give him that satisfaction.

"Guess I was wrong," Gil said when Courtney didn't answer. He blew her a kiss and headed off into the crowd.

Courtney pulled the girls' pizza out to cool and when she shifted around to place it on the counter, she found Graham standing there.

"Hey, Graham," Courtney said, smiling at him. "Did you finally beat Yanoo?"

"Was there a problem with Gil just now?"

"No more than usual," Courtney said. "But I can handle him."

"Good," he said, and turned to leave.

"Graham," Courtney called out. When he turned, Courtney said, "Thanks for asking, though."

He nodded and headed to the pool table. Courtney

happened to look in Gil's direction. Gil was watching every step Graham made. And the look on his face wasn't friendly.

Great.

This was the first time Graham had shown up.

And Courtney could already smell disaster.

GRAHAM STOOD AT the pool table, waiting for his next shot. He'd never told Courtney about the conversation he'd had with Gil. But he had told Yanoo. And though this was the first time he'd personally been able to show up on a Friday night, Yanoo had kept a close eye on Gil's visits.

According to Yanoo, so far Courtney hadn't had a problem putting Gil in his place. Still, Graham didn't trust him. And he didn't trust what Gil might do now that Graham was here.

"Listen up, people."

Graham looked up from the shot he was ready to make and frowned when he saw the very guy he'd been thinking about standing on the stage with the microphone in his hand. Graham knocked the ball into the side pocket with a loud thud, the same way he would knock Gil out if he laid a hand on Courtney.

"I just wanted to remind everyone the Woodsman contest is next weekend," Gil said. "The contest is still open for registration, people. And I look forward to seeing if anyone is man enough to take my title this year."

Gil reached out to place the microphone on the stand. Then he stopped and brought the mike back to his mouth. "I forgot to mention all of the proceeds go to local island charities, folks, and the age limit to enter is from eighteen to eighty. So for all you old rich guys like Graham back there playing pool, just because you no longer have what it takes to enter the contest doesn't mean we're not happy to take your donation."

"Hey, Graham," someone called out, "The cocky little SOB just singled you out. Enter the contest and make him regret the day he called you old."

Every eye in the store looked in Graham's direction.

"I thought Gil's insult was calling me rich," Graham yelled back. "He knows I'm still young enough to kick his butt any day of the week."

The crowd went wild.

When the noise died down, Gil brought the microphone back to his mouth and said, "Care to make a side bet you won't make it past round one, Graham?"

"As long as the money still goes to charity, you name the bet, Gil."

"One thousand dollars says you won't see round two."

"Deal. As long as you double that amount when I take your title for myself."

An instant hush fell across the crowd. Then everyone started talking at once.

Gil left the stage with a smug grin on his face. And Graham returned to his pool game. But he definitely wasn't smiling. Inside, Graham was seething. Gil had made him pay for demanding he leave Courtney alone.

He'd taken their quarrel public.

But he'd picked the wrong guy's chain to rattle.

Graham finished making a shot and started to line up another when Courtney approached the pool table. The expression on her face matched the fire in her eyes.

"I thought you were drinking beer tonight."

"I am drinking beer tonight," Graham said, nodding toward his cooler in the corner. "Want one?"

"It sounded like you've been drinking straight testosterone to me." Now her arms were crossed.

Not a good sign.

"Just a little harmless bantering." Graham took aim and made another shot.

"Tell me the truth, Graham. What's going on?"

Graham walked to the other side of the pool table.

Courtney followed him.

"Why don't you ask Gil? He started it."

"I don't want to ask Gil," she said. "I'm asking you."

"Leave it alone, Courtney."

"I'm waiting for an honest answer, Graham."

"I am being honest," Graham said. "Leave it alone."

COURTNEY DIDN'T leave it alone. She cornered Gil the second she found him.

Gil hesitated at first, then he said, "You know I'm crazy about you, Courtney. So don't force me into telling you something that I know is going to hurt your feelings."

"I'm a big girl. I'm sure I can take it."

"You want to know why I still keep coming on Friday nights even though you won't go out with me? I'll tell you why. You're wasting your time waiting around for Graham, and I was hoping you'd finally realize that. I asked Graham straight up if he was interested in you before I ever asked you out. And you know what the arrogant ass said? Not in a million years."

Courtney swallowed. "Graham really said that?"

"Those were his exact words. Not in a million years."

Courtney knew Gil was lying. She could see it in his eyes.

More than that Graham would never say such a thing, especially not to Gil. Graham would never disrespect her by saying *not in a million years.*

"That's why I called Graham out," Gil said. "I should have kicked his ass before. Now I can do it in front of the whole town."

"So? Does that mean you're going to ask me to go out with you again?"

Gil grinned. "Absolutely. Will you please go out with me, Courtney?"

"Not in a million years."

His eyes turned cold. "Bitch."

Courtney walked away before she slapped him. She also felt like slapping Graham.

She couldn't believe Graham had let Gil goad him into entering some macho nonsense contest. But the fact that Graham had told her to leave it alone made Courtney realize there was more to the story than she knew.

If Graham wouldn't tell her, Courtney knew someone who would. And as soon as she got the opportunity, she would ask Yanoo.

Courtney had just walked back to the grill when Gil marched out the door with his cooler under his arm. She guessed this would be Gil's last Friday night visit, and for that, Courtney was thankful.

She looked around for Graham.

Now he, too, was headed for the door, although he did wave before he left.

Courtney didn't even try to stop him. Instead she tracked down Yanoo where he was propped up against the wall, drinking a beer and watching while two of the other locals played pool. When he saw Courtney walking toward him, he met her halfway.

"Are you willing to tell me what's going on?"

"You need to hear that from Graham," he said.

"And you just heard Graham tell me to leave it alone. Please, Yanoo. I'm completely baffled why Graham would let Gil goad him into some stupid contest that could get him hurt."

"It's a matter of honor," Yanoo said. "Gil called Graham out in front of the whole town. He can't let Gil shame him like that."

"Well, that's plain stupid," Courtney said. "Everyone in town knows what an ass Gil is. And bringing himself down to Gil's level only makes Graham look like an ass, too. And I intend to tell Graham that."

Courtney started to walk away.

"No," Yanoo said and grabbed her arm, stopping her.

"It's deeper than that for Graham," Yanoo said. "He lost his self-respect over Julia's death. Let him get it back. Even if Gil is the way he has to do that. Do what Graham told you, Courtney. Leave it alone."

CHAPTER NINETEEN

SINCE THE STANDOFF between Graham and Gil, Courtney hadn't seen Graham at all. He'd had a fishing party at the lodge.

That meant Courtney also hadn't seen much of Rachel. But the lodge guests were gone now, and Rachel was spending the entire day at the store as well as spending the night with Courtney tonight.

The first week in August was already here. Three more weeks and Courtney would be making plans to leave for New York. She and Rachel didn't have much more time to spend together.

After the store closed, Tiki and Hanya were coming over for a girls' night in to help put finishing touches on the jewelry for their wish baskets.

It had been Rachel's idea to use glass beads and tiny pearls for their bracelets and their hair combs. According to Rachel it wouldn't have seemed right unless they decorated their jewelry with the same type of gems their own ancestors had worn.

Courtney had ordered a ton of beads and pearls and jewelry-making supplies from an online craft store, and she hadn't spared any expense. She hoped Rachel really would wear the jewelry they were making together on her wedding day. And if Courtney had anything to do with it, she would be there, carefully placing those combs in Rachel's beautiful black hair.

She glanced at Rachel, envisioning what a beautiful bride Rachel would make someday. At the moment, they were busy slicing tomatoes and getting ready for the daily lunch rush that would descend upon them within the hour.

"You know the whole town's talking about the big fight Dad and Gil had over you, right?"

"Who told you that?"

"Tiki." Rachel reached across Courtney for another tomato. "Tiki said Gil's been telling everyone that Dad threatened him over you, telling him to back off and leave you alone. And Gil is saying he hopes he and Dad will be the last men standing when they reach the final round."

Courtney grimaced.

"Gil's bragging he's going to show Dad why an old man shouldn't let his mouth override his ass."

"Rachel!" Courtney scolded.

"What? I'm just repeating what Gil said."

Rachel waited for Courtney to argue.

When Courtney didn't, Rachel said, "You realize what all of this means, don't you?"

"Yes," Courtney said and sighed. "It means someone is going to get hurt."

"Forget the stupid Woodsman contest, Courtney. It means if Dad won't even let you have a boyfriend, I don't need a freaking wish basket. The chance of a guy even getting near me is *zero.*"

Courtney had to laugh. "Don't ever say you aren't a normal teenager again, Rachel Morrison. Only normal teenagers have the ability to make everything going on around them all about them."

Rachel rolled her eyes.

Graham chose that moment to walk into the store.

"Too early to get a burger around here?" he asked as he sat down at the counter.

"Never too early for you, Graham," Courtney said.

"Courtney's only saying that because she's afraid it might be your last burger," Rachel said.

"Rachel!" Courtney scolded.

"I think I'll go take Broadway out," Rachel said.

"I think that's your best idea today," Courtney told her.

Rachel walked around the counter, but she frowned at her dad as she walked by him. Graham sent Courtney a puzzled look after his daughter left.

"What was that all about?"

Courtney ignored the question. "You like your burgers well-done, right?" She turned around and took a patty from the freezer and put it on the grill.

"You didn't answer my question."

"I could always tell you to leave it alone."

"But?"

"Rachel's been hearing the rumors going around town about you and Gil."

"Gil has a big mouth," Graham said. "But Rachel doesn't have to worry about me."

Courtney laughed. "Rachel isn't worried about you. She's afraid if you won't let me have a boyfriend, she's doomed for life."

"Is that what you think? That I told Gil to back off because I didn't want you to have a boyfriend?"

"Did you tell Gil to back off?

"Yes, I did."

"Then maybe I should ask why you would care if I had a boyfriend." She tried to sound calm even though her heart was pounding. His response shouldn't mean this much, but it did.

"I didn't want *Gil* trying to become your boyfriend. That was the problem."

"You can't possibly think I would ever be interested in Gil, Graham. If you do, you don't even know who I am."

"Of course, I didn't think you would be interested in Gil. But he isn't used to women turning him down."

Courtney blinked. "You mean you think Gil—"

"I don't know what Gil would have done if you'd turned him down when you were alone. That's why I told him to back off."

Courtney thought about what Graham said as she finished assembling his burger. She'd seen Gil's face when he called her a bitch. And she remembered briefly thinking she was glad the store was filled with people.

"You should be prepared for the rumors to get worse as the week goes on. That's Gil's trademark. He likes to talk about women. And none of it is ever flattering."

Courtney walked to the cooler, grabbed a drink for both of them then sat beside him at the counter. "If that's true, and you think Gil will spread lies about me, what are we going to do about Rachel?"

Graham put his burger down and looked at her. "I hadn't thought about that. Maybe you should warn her that might happen."

Courtney nodded in agreement. She was pleased that Graham trusted her enough to have such a talk with Rachel. She'd given Rachel a lot of advice over the summer. But she was no longer giving Rachel advice she didn't take herself.

Since the night she'd had her breakdown on Beth and called her mother, she'd been talking with her mother on a regular basis. And although they were only taking baby steps, each step they took brought them closer to having a good mother-daughter relationship instead of having no relationship at all.

That's what she wanted for Graham and Rachel—a good father-daughter relationship. And if she left with nothing more than knowing she'd had a part in helping them achieve that, it would be enough.

Comforted somewhat by that lie, Courtney got through the lunch hour. After cleaning up she walked to where Rachel was restocking the canned vegetables shelf. "I think we need to talk about these rumors you've been hearing about your dad and Gil."

"What about them?" Rachel bent and picked up two more cans of peas from the box sitting on the floor beside her.

"I just wanted to make sure you knew that your dad isn't the bad guy in this situation."

Rachel looked surprised. "But I thought you liked Gil. He's always flirting with you."

"I thought I did, too," Courtney said. "But I was never interested in sleeping with him. And Gil didn't like being turned down."

"Wow," Rachel said. "I can't believe you said that. We've never talked about sex before."

"Maybe it's time we did," Courtney said.

"And that's all Gil wanted? Sex?"

"That's the only thing guys like Gil ever want, Rachel."

"And my dad's the good guy because...?"

"Because your dad knows who Gil is, and he was trying to protect me."

Rachel grinned. "And what if my dad wanted to have sex with you? Would that make him the bad guy?"

No, that would be a miracle.

"Sex isn't the issue, Rachel. A person's integrity is the issue. Men like Gil have no scruples when it comes to women. They pretend to be interested until they get what they want, then they move on. And sometimes when they don't get what they want, they lie and say they did. So it's possible you might hear some other rumors, and they might be ugly. But you have my word right now that none of them will be true. Okay?"

"Okay."

"And that's the difference between guys like Gil and guys like your dad. Sex only enters into the situation for a guy like your dad when they are interested in a woman."

"Then I guess that means my dad will never have sex again. He isn't interested in anyone but himself."

"Now, see, that's where you're wrong," Courtney said. "Your dad told Gil to back off because he was interested in protecting me. Your dad is an honorable man. There are a lot worse things than having an honorable man in your life, Rachel. I promise you that."

Rachel frowned. "Why are you always taking up for my dad?"

"Because I want you to see him for who he really is. He loves you. And even though you think his rules are stupid and his decision to live here is only to punish you, you're wrong. When you have children of your own one day, you'll understand why he did a lot of the things he did. He has your best interest at heart."

"Forget children," Rachel said. "I'm still waiting for my first boyfriend."

Me, too.

YANOO WAS SITTING ON his porch when Graham pulled the skiff up to the dock. With the girls all gathered at the store for their girls' night in, sitting outside on the porch with Yanoo was the closest Graham could come to a boys' night out.

He grabbed the six-pack of beer and headed for the porch. Thirty minutes later neither he nor Yanoo had said a word. Graham had sat sipping his beer. Yanoo had continued carving the whalebone that was beginning to resemble the head of a raven.

"Am I doing the right thing?" Graham finally asked.

"About Gil or about Courtney?"

"About Gil," Graham said, bringing his bottle to his lips again. "I'm not ready to hear your latest opinion about Courtney."

"Gil has a loud mouth," Yanoo said. "It's time someone shut it for him."

"He's also ten years younger than I am."

"Any contest is a mind-over-matter challenge. You aren't insecure. Gil is."

Graham looked over at him. "Why do you say Gil's insecure?"

"The Woodsman title. The women. The bragging. Gil's still trying to prove he's a man. You have nothing to prove."

They sat in silence until the beer was gone and Yanoo had finished the carving. Graham made no move to get up.

Yanoo made no mention that Graham should leave. They were both waiting for the question that still remained.

"So...Courtney?"

"Look deep inside your heart for that answer."

"And if I'm afraid of what I find?"

"Look deeper," Yanoo said, "until you find the strength to accept what you know is true."

"Tell me something. Do you love Hanya as much as you did when you married her?"

"No. I love her more."

Graham sighed. "It didn't work that way for me."

"But Courtney isn't Julia."

"And you don't think I know that?"

Yanoo shrugged. "Then why compare the relationship you had in the past to the one you're still trying to avoid now?"

Graham picked up his carton of empty bottles and headed for the skiff. He didn't have to look behind him to know Yanoo would watch from the porch until he was safely on his way.

His boys' night out was over.

But his dilemma over Courtney wasn't.

He didn't care what Yanoo said, he'd been married. And when the honeymoon was over, people changed. Courtney had proved she could live in Port Protection. She even seemed happy here, but she also knew she was only staying for the summer. A nagging thought wouldn't leave Graham alone. How long would Courtney stay happy in Port Protection if he admitted he loved her and asked her to stay forever?

As for looking deep inside his heart?

He didn't have to look deep to know he loved her.

Every time he breathed he knew he loved Courtney.

It was the strength to accept what he knew was true that Graham was still searching for.

CHAPTER TWENTY

IF GRAHAM HAD ANY doubts about staying in the Woodsman contest, those doubts were gone by the time the competition arrived. As he'd predicted, new rumors were flying fast and furious.

And none of them were good.

But human nature was human nature, even on secluded Prince of Wales Island. So the contest that usually drew only a small number of onlookers with nothing more exciting to do on a Saturday afternoon had turned into a record-breaking crowd with people coming from every direction.

Graham headed for the store as soon as he reached town to see how Courtney was holding up. She'd had enough class not to dignify Gil's lies by bothering to deny them, but he knew she was embarrassed nonetheless.

People who knew Courtney knew they were lies. People who didn't know her didn't matter. He'd reminded her of that, and hoped she'd listened.

When Graham walked through the door at three o'clock, the store was packed. People were everywhere, filling up their coolers, picking out their snacks, all getting ready for the start at four.

Courtney looked up and saw him. Graham ignored

the stares and the whispers and headed straight for the lunch counter where she worked. He nodded toward the back of the store when he reached the counter. Courtney finished what she was doing and followed.

"Are you okay?"

Courtney sighed and said, "Aside from the snide glances and strangers filing in and out to get a good look at me, yes. I'm okay. Are you?"

"We'll both be better at the end of the day," Graham said, nodding toward Rachel, who was still working behind the lunch counter and not looking one bit happy about it. "And Rachel?"

"She's still angry that I'm making her work instead of going to the contest, but she'll get over it."

"I owe you for keeping Rachel here."

"Then return the favor by coming back to get your daughter in one piece."

"That's a promise."

He left and walked toward the town square to sign in and pick up his contest number. Yanoo was right. This was a mind-over-matter challenge. When it came down to who won and who lost any competition, it wasn't only skill that prevailed. It was the winner's ability to keep a cool head.

Graham knew he had that ability.

He was counting on the fact that Gil didn't.

THE BARLOW TWINS walked into the store each holding a handle of the large cooler positioned between them. Courtney hurried in their direction and pulled the twins aside. "Are you going to the contest?"

They looked at each other, then back at Courtney.

"You're kidding, right?" they said in unison.

"Oh, stop being smart-asses," Courtney told them. "I have a proposition for you. You can fill your cooler with anything you want free of charge, as long as one of you will come back during the competition with updates."

"Deal," they both said, and hurried off.

That problem solved, Courtney walked to the cash register and took money from two older men she'd never seen before. They stepped away from the counter and opened the cold drinks they'd just purchased.

"It might be a toss-up in the wood splitting competition," the shorter man said. "I hear Morrison is favored to win that event."

Courtney's heart sank. As much as she wanted Graham to earn back his self-respect, she couldn't help but secretly wish he wouldn't make it through to the second round. And she'd already decided if Graham did lose his thousand-dollar bet to Gil, she would be the one paying the money, and she wasn't going to argue about it. Besides the fact that Graham was in this contest because of her, he also had credited her debit card when she tried to pay him for the plane ticket and staying at the lodge. She wouldn't let him get away with turning her money down a second time.

"The ax throw is Gil's best event," the taller of the two men said. "He hit the bull's-eye with all five throws last year. That's why he's been the champion for the last four years."

"Yeah," the short guy said, "but Gil fights dirty. He almost put that guy's eye out year before last."

The men walked off as Courtney's stomach rolled over.

It totally irritated her to think that this was the twenty-first century and men still felt the need to participate in barbaric rituals that should have been outlawed ages ago. Why couldn't the final event have been something more civilized? A footrace, for instance, instead of two men willing to slam each other to the ground and punch and gouge and who knew what else in an effort to prove that one man was stronger than the other.

It just didn't make any sense.

Courtney looked up and suddenly realized there wasn't a customer left in the store. When she looked toward the lunch counter, Rachel was staring right at her, arms crossed defiantly, one black eyebrow raised in question.

"Well?" Rachel said with a smirk. "Think we should hire an extra employee to help us with all of these customers?"

"People will trickle in and out all day," Courtney said. "We both need to be here when they do."

"And between trickles?"

We wait for news that Graham is okay.

"We do what we do any other day, Rachel. We clean, we stock shelves and we keep busy. That's our job."

"Well, that just plain sucks!" Rachel declared.

Courtney agreed.

The entire situation just plain sucked.

GRAHAM POSITIONED HIS hands one above the other on the long-handled ax, and the thought crossed his mind that he was glad Rachel hadn't bought him the wood splitter for his birthday back in May. He also found it ironic, however, that the present Rachel had surprised him with was the reason he was standing in the middle of town square as a contestant in the Woodsman competition now.

"Axes ready," Snag Horton, with his big gold front tooth, called out as he raised the revolver into the air.

Graham raised the ax above his head.

He didn't look to the left or the right at his opponents. Nor had he engaged in conversation with anyone after he arrived in the town square.

He'd let Gil do all the talking. And he'd ignored Gil completely when he kept making wisecracks about Graham's age that caused chuckles from some of the bystanders, and dirty looks from a majority of people who had the strong desire to see Gil get his ass kicked before the day was over.

Mind over matter.

Graham focused on the piece of wood sitting on the stump in front of him. He was looking for the sweet spot, searching for the exact place in the center of the wood that would give him a clean split.

"On your mark. Get set. Go!" Snag yelled and pulled the trigger.

Graham's ax came down and split the wood in half.

COURTNEY JUMPED UP from the stool at the lunch counter when Mark Barlow barreled through the front door with a big grin on his face. "Graham just won the wood splitting competition," he said proudly. "And get this, Gil came in third. He barely made it to round two. And, man, was he pissed about it."

Mark slammed back out the door.

So Graham had won the first round. Gil had lost his thousand dollars. And all Courtney could do was pray

Graham didn't make it through to the next round and the whole thing would be over.

"Big deal," Rachel said, when Courtney looked over at her. "Dad spends half his life splitting wood. It *should* have been a piece of cake for Dad to win that round."

"Speaking of a piece of cake," Courtney said, suddenly badly in need of comfort food, "there's still one piece left of that cherry cheesecake I made that you love. Want to share it with me?"

"I can't," Rachel snipped. "I have this annoying slave driver boss who insists that I keep busy."

Rachel marched toward the pool table with her broom.

"Keep being such a witch," Courtney called after her, "and you'll be riding that broom by the end of the day."

"*Not* funny."

GRAHAM COULD SEE GIL from the corner of his eye, lining up his five short-handled axes on the table in front of him like a skilled surgeon preparing for a major operation. They were all expensive competition axes; all balanced perfectly, blades sharpened to a gleam, grips on the handles for better precision.

Graham looked down at the five short-handled axes he had lined up on his table. One ax was his own from his storage shed. Two he'd borrowed from Yanoo. One belonged to Fat Man Jack sitting behind Graham in the spectator area—except Fat Man Jack was sitting on two folding chairs to hold his massive frame. And the last ax had belonged to Graham's grandfather.

His grandfather's ax was one he rarely used.

But Graham couldn't think of a better time than now.

In this round, Graham and the other three contestants

had drawn numbers to determine in what order they threw. Graham had drawn number one, the worst spot to be in. Gil would go last, meaning Gil would know exactly how many points he needed to win.

Graham focused on the target straight ahead of him, twenty feet away. He already knew Gil had made a perfect score during last year's competition. So did everyone else. Gil had spent the past fifteen minutes making sure everyone knew about his perfect score.

The umpire signaled for Graham to get ready.

Graham picked up his first ax. When he stepped to the throw line, an immediate hush fell over the crowd.

Graham took aim, drew back his arm and threw.

Cheers erupted when the ax hit the bull's-eye.

COURTNEY KEPT LOOKING at her watch. It seemed like hours since Mark had come to report that Graham had won the first round.

The bell on the door sounded.

Courtney held her breath.

But a woman with two small children walked into the store. "Do you have a bathroom we could use?"

"Sure," Courtney said, and pointed to the far side of the store.

"Twenty dollars says they won't buy a single thing," Rachel grumbled when the bathroom door closed.

Courtney started to comment, but Clark burst through the front door.

"Graham just won the ax-throw," he shouted.

Rachel dropped her broom. "Shut the f—front door," she finished when Courtney's head jerked in her direction.

"I'm telling you," Clark said, "the crowd out there is

freaking jumping, man." He held up four fingers. "Four. That's how many times Graham hit the bull's-eye."

"And Gil?" Courtney asked, praying Gil hadn't advanced.

"Gil only hit the bull's-eye three times," Clark said. "And you should have seen him. Threw a fit. He even claimed something was wrong with his target and made the umpire check it. Believe me, Gil did not like coming in second to Graham in his best event."

Clark grinned and did a wide stir-the-pot hip roll.

"It's on, baby," he said. "This competition is *on!*"

GRAHAM TAPPED the right heel of his boot against the left, and the left heel against the right, freeing the attached spurs from any loose debris. He held his arms out so Yanoo could tighten the halter belt around his waist.

"You could end this now and still accomplish all you need to do," Yanoo said. "You've already hurt Gil's pride. You've won his best event. And you've put a big dent in his bank account."

"His bank account isn't what I came to put a dent in. You've heard the lies he's told about Courtney. Would you quit now if he'd spread that filth about Hanya?"

"Then you only have to hit somewhere between Gil's time and the guy in second place," Yanoo said. "You don't have to win this event."

Yanoo ran the leather strap around the thirty-five-foot pole that had been set up in the middle of the town square and fastened the clip to Graham's belt. Graham took a minute to roll his shoulders and relieve the tension at the base of his neck. He grabbed both sides of the strap, sliding it up and down to make sure it was loose enough to slide up the pole and tight enough to bear his weight.

Gil had already scaled the pole and stopped the timer at the top at nineteen seconds. Twenty-two seconds had been the time for the guy in second place. Both men were younger. But youth wasn't everything. Determination was.

Graham signaled he was ready.

The gun fired.

Graham took off up the pole.

MARK STAGGERED through the door, out of breath from running. He bent over, his hands on his knees, trying to catch his breath.

"What?" Courtney demanded. "Tell me what happened."

Mark finally straightened, holding up a finger, still unable to talk. "Graham..." He took in another big gulp of air.

"Mark!" Courtney begged. "Tell me."

"Graham didn't win the pole climb," he finally managed to say. "But he came in second. He and Gil are squaring off now for the wrestling match."

Courtney whirled around to face Rachel. "You stay here. I can't take this anymore."

Courtney ran past Mark and out the door.

Rachel ran out the door right behind her.

Broadway loped off after both of them.

CHAPTER TWENTY-ONE

WHEN COURTNEY AND RACHEL reached the town square it was so crowded they couldn't see a thing. But the loud shouts coming from the circle that had formed to watch the last event told Courtney the wrestling match was already underway.

"We've got to get closer," Courtney told Rachel, taking her hand and starting through the crowd.

"Wait, there's Yanoo," Rachel said, pulling Courtney to a stop and pointing in the opposite direction.

Courtney took the lead, tugging Rachel with her as they made their way toward the tallest man in the crowd. When they finally reached where Yanoo was standing, he stepped aside ushering them and Broadway in front of him, where Tiki and Hanya were already standing.

"*Unfreakingbelievable,*" Rachel said as she slid in beside Tiki.

Broadway whined.

And Courtney gasped.

Graham and Gil were stripped down to the waist, circling each other. Gil's lip was bleeding. Graham had a gash above his right eye.

Gil lowered his head and charged. Graham took the

head butt straight to the stomach. Courtney turned her back, unable to watch.

"Pin him, Dad!" Rachel yelled out. "Pin his sorry ass to the ground."

"Rachel Elizabeth Morrison!" Courtney exclaimed.

But Rachel was too busy watching her father, who now had Gil on the ground, Gil's head in a headlock and both of Gil's shoulders only inches from the ground.

HAD IT NOT BEEN FOR the screaming crowd, someone might have heard what Graham said when he tightened his grip around Gil's neck and brought Gil's right ear close to his mouth. "Here's the deal. I can pin you right now and we both know it. Or you can make a public apology to Courtney and keep your title. It's your choice."

"Okay, okay," Gil grunted.

Graham loosened his grip.

Gil flipped over and pinned Graham to the ground.

THANK GOD, IT'S OVER was Courtney's first thought.

Gil and Graham stood, shook hands and the official overseeing the event stepped forward. Gil waved to the crowd as the official held up Gil's right hand, declaring him the Tongass National Forest Woodsman champion for the fifth straight year.

Courtney couldn't stomach watching Gil gloat over keeping his title. She started walking away with the rest of the crowd that was already breaking up.

"Courtney, wait."

Courtney stopped walking at the sound of her name.

The crowd stopped walking when they saw who said it.

Courtney turned to see Gil heading toward her.

"I owe you an apology," Gil said, loud enough for everyone to hear. "You wouldn't sleep with me, and it pissed me off. And when Graham told me to leave you alone, that pissed me off. I said things about you that weren't true. I'm sorry for doing that."

"Thank you." But her mind was busy with the realization that Graham let Gil win.

He'd let Gil keep his title in exchange for an apology. And that was the difference between guys like Graham and guys like Gil.

Graham was a real man.

Gil never would be.

Courtney looked across the square. Rachel had her arms around Graham's neck, giving him a big hug. She started to walk over to join them, then saw Graham was leaving. He didn't even look in her direction. He just headed off through the crowd.

Courtney sighed and walked the other way. She had just reached the store when Rachel ran up, Tiki and Broadway right behind her. "Am I still sentenced to more boss abuse, or can I go home with Tiki now?"

Courtney knew Rachel already had plans to spend the night with Tiki. "What did your dad say?"

"Dad said it was up to you. He's going home to take a shower. He said he was done for the day."

Done for the day.

"Your sentence is over," Courtney said. "Have a good time."

Rachel and Tiki headed off.

Courtney looked down at Broadway. "I guess it's going to be just you and me for the night, buddy."

AFTER GIL MADE the apology to Courtney, all Graham had wanted was to get away from everyone as fast as possible. He was mentally and physically drained.

He pulled the skiff up to the lodge's dock, secured the boat and walked up the path, headed straight for the shower. His gash on his forehead hurt like a son of a bitch, but at least his pride didn't.

He'd done the right thing letting Gil keep his title.

And no one had to know. Graham knew. That was all that mattered.

Walking into his bathroom, Graham stripped before he leaned close to the bathroom mirror, inspecting the gash. But when he stepped back from the mirror, he looked at his reflection for a long time.

And that's when Graham realized the man staring back at him wasn't the same man he'd been five years ago. He also wasn't too weak to admit what he really wanted.

He wanted Courtney.

He'd wanted her from the first time he saw her.

He'd want her until he took his last breath.

COURTNEY KNEW IT was stupid, but she had actually expected Graham to come to the store after he'd showered. The fact that he didn't was more than a letdown. It was the ending of the final chapter of the going-nowhere saga Beth called *Courtney, Hopelessly in Love.*

Love from Alaska wasn't going to happen for her.

She'd been a fool to ever think it would.

Courtney checked her watch and her spirits sank even lower. It was eight o'clock, one hour past the time she usually closed the store. Yet she'd been stupid enough to remain sitting here waiting to hear the bell ring above the door, and to see Graham come walking into the store. Well, the bell wasn't ringing. And she was tired of waiting.

Two weeks and counting. Her time was running out fast.

And no one seemed to notice but her.

Her quickly approaching departure date reminded Courtney that she still hadn't talked to Graham on Rachel's behalf about Peg and Hal's anniversary party. Rachel even had all of the details already worked out. She would go to Seattle with Courtney, and she could return with Peg and Hal.

Courtney would make it a point to talk to Graham tomorrow. Even if it meant going to the lodge to do it.

Courtney walked to the front door, flipped the sign on the door to Closed then locked the front door. That's when Broadway whined.

"Ten minutes," Courtney told him as she let him out. "No longer. That's how long I'll need to run my bath."

Courtney closed the door and headed for the spiral staircase, flipping off the downstairs lights as she went. She'd take a long, hot bubble bath, maybe drink a little wine, then she'd get a good night's sleep.

She deserved it after the day she'd had.

GRAHAM STOOD ON the dock below The Wooden Nickel, relieved to see the downstairs lights were off and the store was closed. He'd been standing here for several minutes now, rehearsing everything he planned to say.

He'd told Courtney once to go home. That what she

was looking for wasn't here. The day he said it, that statement had been true.

But a lot had changed since then.

He loved her. He loved Courtney, mind, body and soul. And tonight he planned to tell her that.

Graham patted his shirt pocket, making sure the small black velvet box with his grandmother Morrison's pearl and diamond ring was still there. Then Graham took a deep breath and started up the steps with the same determination that had gotten him through the Woodsman contest. Broadway met him on the top landing.

"Wish me luck, boy."

Graham had his hand poised and ready to knock when the door suddenly opened and Courtney gasped.

"You scared me," she said, clutching the front of her silky robe together as Broadway trotted inside.

They stared at each other.

"I've changed my mind," Graham said. "And if you tell me it's too late, I don't blame you. But I'm begging you not to do that. I love you, Courtney. I love you for believing in me when I didn't believe in myself. And I love you for staying when I told you to go home. I guess the question is, do you love me?"

"Completely," Courtney said.

Graham dropped down on one knee right there in the doorway, pulled the box out of his pocket and opened it for Courtney to see. "Then say you'll marry me. Marry me at the gazebo and let me prove what you're looking for is here."

EVERY HOPE, EVERY WISH, every dream was right here in front of her, waiting. All Courtney had to do was reach out and make it real. And so she did.

"Yes," Courtney said. "I'll marry you."

Graham slipped the ring on her finger. "This is a family heirloom handed down to my grandmother. But if you want your own ring, I'll understand."

"No," Courtney said. "It's beautiful."

Graham stood and kissed her. And Courtney knew her long wait for Graham to change his mind had been well worth it. She took him by the hand and did what she'd fantasized about doing every time she looked at him. She led him up the spiral staircase to the loft overhead.

They barely made it past the top step before Graham had her in his arms. He pushed the robe off her shoulders and let it fall to the floor. And Courtney couldn't get his clothes off fast enough.

They made love right where they were. On the floor. Teasing each other, tasting each other and touching each other everywhere at once.

Graham had her legs over his shoulders, pounding into her, as eager for his own release as she was for hers. And when they both finally cried out with pleasure, they did it all over again.

Courtney would never get enough of Graham.

Not in a night.

Not in a year.

Not in a lifetime.

She would never get enough of Graham.

GRAHAM WASN'T SURE HOW they ended up in Hal and Peg's big claw-foot bathtub. He was still reeling from the most incredible sex of his life—the kind of sex where you find yourself on the floor, so hungry for each other that nothing else matters.

But all Graham cared about now was the incredible feel of Courtney's breasts, wet and slick with soap, as she sat astride him bringing him closer and closer to another climax.

Graham let his hands slide from her breasts down to her hips, trying to slow her pace, but it only increased her urgency. She was moving faster and faster, driving him so crazy Graham said those words out loud.

He felt her body stiffen as she arched her back.

Next, her whole body shuddered.

She leaned forward and kissed the cut on his forehead softly, then his neck, taking tiny little nibbles with her teeth that made him moan. She was still sitting astride him, still rocking back and forth against him, still making him grow harder with every movement she made.

Her lips moved to his ear.

Slowly, she sucked his earlobe into her mouth.

Graham gripped her hips tighter, holding her still now, thrusting deeper and deeper inside her as he sought his own release. She pulled back, holding on to his forearms, matching him thrust for thrust as he cried out her name.

Again, they climaxed together.

She leaned forward and whispered, "More."

And Graham knew he would die a happy man.

COURTNEY HELD ON TO the iron railing of the headboard on the bed and bit down hard on her lower lip as Graham parted her legs and lowered his head. She moaned with pleasure when his hot tongue slid inside her. His hands slipped beneath her hips, bringing her flush against his mouth as his tongue darted in and out.

Courtney held on and rode the wave.

Faster.

And faster.

Closer.

And closer.

Until she exploded inside with a massive shiver.

Graham slowly kissed his way up her body.

"More?" he said, balancing himself above her on his hands.

Courtney grinned. "I think I'm good for now."

"Thank God," he said, flopping over on his back. "You forget I'm an old man."

"*My* old man," Courtney corrected, resting her head on Graham's shoulder.

He kissed her forehead and brought her fingers up to his lips. Courtney sighed, looking at the beautiful white pearl and the diamonds twinkling at her from the moonlight shining through the bedroom window.

She was engaged.

Oh. My. God.

She was actually engaged.

CHAPTER TWENTY-TWO

WHEN COURTNEY HAD first opened her eyes on Sunday morning, it was barely first light. She'd been lying in bed for almost an hour now, watching Graham sleep and thinking about how much she loved him.

She'd been thinking about a million other things, too. Such as how she was going to convince her uptown mother to attend a wedding in the wilds of Alaska and ride in a skiff to a gazebo in the middle of nowhere for the ceremony. Beth would be her maid of honor, of course. And Yanoo would be Graham's best man.

Rachel and Tiki would make beautiful bridesmaids, and Rachel would be so proud when she helped arrange the combs in Courtney's hair that they'd made together for her wish basket. And Hanya could be in charge of her bride's book. And she couldn't forget Broadway—he could act as the ring-bearer. She'd seen a dog do that in some movie once.

They'd have the reception at The Wooden Nickel and invite the whole town, and…

Graham stirred beside her. He opened his eyes.

When he found her staring at him, he smiled. "How long have you been awake?"

"Long enough to work out most of the details of our wedding," Courtney said happily.

He pulled her to him and put his arm around her. Courtney snuggled against him, running her hand up and down his muscled chest.

"And have you picked a wedding date?" he asked.

"I thought that was one detail we should decide together," Courtney told him.

"How about this coming weekend?" he said. "It only takes three days to get a license in Alaska."

Courtney laughed.

He leaned forward. "Should I take that as a no?"

Courtney propped herself up on her elbow and looked at him. "Of course, that's a no, Graham. I don't want to get married without my friends and family here. And I would think you would feel the same way."

"My friends and family are here," he said.

"Not all of your family. Your parents aren't here. Don't you want to invite your parents to attend our wedding?"

"No."

"May I ask why?"

"No."

Courtney sat up in bed and said, "Well, excuse me, but I don't consider that an acceptable answer. You claim you want to spend the rest of your life with me, yet you don't see the need to tell me why you wouldn't want to invite your parents to our wedding?"

"Because they wouldn't come to a wedding here, okay? Instead they'd want us to have the wedding in New York, where they could make a big production of things."

"Then I have another question for you. Rachel really wants to go with me to Hal and Peg's anniversary party in Seattle. Will you let her go?"

"I'll think about it," Graham said.

Courtney couldn't keep herself from asking, "You'll think about it seriously? Or like you were going to think about letting Rachel go to school in Ketchikan or Anchorage?"

He frowned at her. "What's that supposed to mean?"

"It means," Courtney said, "that school will start in a few weeks. And so far you haven't made a move to do anything about it. Don't think Rachel isn't aware of that. She thinks the subject is closed."

Graham sat up in bed. "Well, excuse me if I've been up to my ass in fishermen all summer. I haven't had time to do anything."

"I really want Rachel to go to Seattle with me, Graham. I want you to come, too. It would be a nice change for all of us."

Graham threw the sheet back and got out of bed.

He walked out of the bedroom naked.

Courtney wrapped the sheet around her and followed. When she found him, he was in the bathroom pulling on the boxer shorts he'd left on the bathroom floor.

Graham grabbed his watch sitting on the vanity, slid it onto his arm and pointed a finger at Courtney. "I tried to tell you this would happen," he said. "We've been engaged, what?" He looked down at his watch, then back at her. "We've been engaged almost twelve hours to the minute, and you're already talking about Seattle being a nice change from here."

"A nice change for a *weekend,* Graham," Courtney stressed. "Not permanently."

"My life here *is* permanent, Courtney," he said, "and if you're having doubts about making Port Protection your permanent residence, don't marry me."

"Well, how unbelievably convenient of you, Graham," Courtney said, flipping the sheet to the floor and gathering up the robe she'd left in the bathroom the night before. "We've been engaged—" she grabbed his arm and looked at his watch "—*exactly* twelve hours now and you're already looking for an excuse to get out of marrying me."

Courtney pointed a finger at Graham. "But if you think for one minute just because I love you that I'm going to assume the role of the meek little backwoods housewife and never say a word when I think you're wrong about something, then don't marry me!"

He clenched his jaw. "Why do I get the feeling you aren't just talking about Seattle?"

"You don't want to know."

"I'm asking, aren't I?"

Common sense told Courtney this time she should leave it alone. She'd barely had time to digest that Graham had asked her to marry him. She didn't want him to think now that she'd let him chase her until she caught him that she was changing all the rules. But she had some rules that if Graham couldn't abide by, she needed to know it sooner than later.

Courtney took a deep breath. "I'll be willing to live with you in Port Protection for the rest of our lives, Graham. But I don't intend to be the hermit you've become and never leave the island. If I marry you, you and Rachel will be my family. And that means when I do go to New York or anywhere else, I'll want my family to be with me. If you aren't willing to do that, you need to tell me now."

Graham looked at her for a long time.

"Are you through?"

Courtney nodded.

"So am I."

Courtney slipped his grandmother's ring off her finger and held the ring out for Graham to take. She prayed that he wouldn't take it. That he'd pull her into his arms and take her back to bed and prove to her all over again that what she'd always been looking for was standing right in front of her.

Graham took the ring and walked out of the bathroom.

Courtney let him go.

She jumped at the sound of the front door slamming. Then Courtney slumped onto the floor, unable to believe what had happened.

Twelve hours.

Oh. My. God.

Her engagement had lasted only twelve hours.

GRAHAM STARTED DOWN the long flight of steps leading to the dock, Broadway right beside him. He stopped when he reached the bottom step, turned around and marched right back to the top of the landing, Broadway right beside him.

Graham stood there for a minute.

Broadway whined.

"Oh, shut up," Graham said, "I'm thinking."

Going down the steps, he'd been thinking that he'd done the right thing by taking the ring back. That his gut instinct had told him all along Courtney would start talking about New York the minute he told her he loved her. That he didn't need Courtney telling him how to raise his daughter. And that the chance of Courtney ever turning into some meek little backwoods housewife was as likely as his entering the Woodsman contest again.

But coming up the steps, he'd been thinking that he didn't want a life without Courtney in it. That he respected her for speaking her mind when she thought he was wrong about something. That Rachel loved and needed her as much as he did. And that what she'd said about him becoming a hermit was true.

Graham shook his head.

Love was one complicated son of a bitch!

COURTNEY WAS STILL sitting on the bathroom floor, her back resting against the bathtub, when she heard the door slam again. She didn't even bother getting up.

Whatever Graham had left behind, he could find it for himself.

But when she heard the click of Broadway's toenails on the metal spiral staircase, she decided Graham had only opened the door to let Broadway in. By the time she heard more footsteps on the stairs, Broadway was already licking at the tear running down her cheek.

When Graham walked to the bathroom doorway, Courtney still didn't get up. She pushed Broadway's head away, and he flopped down and put his big head on her lap.

"I've changed my mind," Graham said.

Courtney moved Broadway off her lap and stood.

Graham took a step in her direction.

The love in his eyes told her all she needed to know.

"About?" Courtney said.

She took a step in Graham's direction.

"Life," he said.

They both took a step forward.

Now they were standing nose-to-nose.

"I think we should check out Ketchikan and Anchorage before we go to Seattle." He paused briefly. "And it might be nice if we spent Christmas in New York this year."

Courtney slid her arms around Graham's neck. "And if your wife decides to stay in advertising, but work out of a home office wherever we are at the time?"

"Would I get free advertising for the lodge?"

"No," Courtney said. "But we could trade it out."

Graham kissed her.

Courtney kissed him back. "Anything else?"

"Yes," Graham said. "Will you please get dressed so we can go tell our daughter we're getting married? Rachel is going to totally freak out."

Courtney laughed.

Broadway barked twice in agreement.

"RACHEL, YOUR DAD IS HERE."

Rachel opened one eye. "What time is it?"

"It's time to get up," Hanya said. "Your dad is waiting in the kitchen. He said to be quick about it."

Tiki looked down from the top bunk when her mother left the bedroom. "What do you think is wrong?"

"Who knows," Rachel grumbled, throwing back the covers and getting up. "Dad probably thought up some new chore to add to my punishment."

"How long is this punishment going to last, Rachel?"

"Try for life."

"Poor you."

"No, poor Dad," Rachel said with conviction. "My punishment ends today. I'm telling him so right now."

"This I gotta see."

Tiki hopped down as Rachel jerked off her pajamas and pulled on her shirt and jeans. Seconds later Rachel was in the lead, marching barefoot out of Tiki's bedroom, down the hallway and into the kitchen.

Rachel came to a stop so fast Tiki bumped into her.

Courtney was at the table with Yanoo and her dad.

"Courtney? What are you doing here?"

"I asked Courtney to come," her dad said.

Instantly, Rachel knew not to pick a fight.

Her dad's I'm-upset-with-you stare was her first clue.

"Courtney's been telling me some things I didn't know."

Rachel braced herself. "Like what?"

"For starters, Courtney said you asked her to persuade me to let you go to Hal and Peg's anniversary party."

Busted.

"Yes, Dad, I asked Courtney to talk to you for me. She's leaving for New York from Seattle. I'd really like to be there to say goodbye."

"*And,*" her dad said, "Courtney says you think the subject's closed on checking out schools in Ketchikan and Anchorage."

Rachel crossed her arms. "And why wouldn't I think that? School starts in a few weeks and you haven't mentioned Ketchikan or Anchorage once since you said you'd think about it."

"I'm mentioning it now," he said. "We'll leave a few days early and check out the schools in both places before we go to Seattle to the party."

"We?" Rachel repeated.

"Yes," he said. "I'm going with you."

Rachel wasn't over that shock when he said, "But you and Courtney will have to fight it out over which city you like best. I'm leaving that decision up to my daughter and my wife."

Rachel blinked. "What wife?"

Courtney held her hand out.

Rachel recognized the ring immediately. She wanted to believe what her dad was saying was true. But they'd played this joke on her before. She'd be stupid to fall for it twice.

"Well?" her dad said. "Don't disappoint us, Rachel. This is the part where you're supposed to totally freak out."

After all you've put me through this summer?

Ha!

"Why would I freak out?" Rachel asked with a smirk. "I told you from the beginning you were perfect for each other."

"And the spirit guides made it all happen."

Rachel whirled around. "Oh, no you don't, Tiki. *I'm* responsible for bringing Dad and Courtney together. *Not* you and your spirit guides."

"Stop arguing," Hanya said, stepping between them and turning Rachel and Tiki around in time to see the kiss the happy couple was sharing. "Love is what brought Graham and Courtney together."

Rachel didn't argue with that statement.

Her mind was already spinning toward the future.

Goodbye isolation. Hello world!

Nothing could stop her from having a normal life now.

CHAPTER TWENTY-THREE

Three years later

COURTNEY HELD GRAHAM'S hand as they walked down the path toward the dock, Broadway leading the way. Graham tightened his grip on her hand when the floatplane flew across the cove and made a graceful landing on the water.

"Be civil to Gil," Courtney lectured as they walked onto the dock.

"I'm always civil to Gil."

Broadway ran on ahead of them.

"And be absolutely charming to Rachel's guest, Graham, if you want our daughter to come home for Thanksgiving again next year. We both know how intimidating you can be. Let's show Rachel she can bring anyone home anytime she wants and never have to worry about either of us doing anything other than making her guest feel right at home."

"The guy *will* sleep upstairs," Graham declared. "And that's final."

"Of course, he's going to sleep upstairs," Courtney said. "So there's no reason to tell the poor boy that he's sleeping upstairs the second he steps off the plane. You'll embarrass Rachel to death."

The plane eased up to the dock.

Broadway barked and wagged his tail.

Courtney slid her arm around Graham's waist as he put his arm around her shoulder. "Smile and look happy," she told him.

"Seems like I've heard that before," Graham grumbled.

The second Rachel stepped out of the plane she dropped down and grabbed Broadway in a big hug. She straightened and waved, then reached for her boyfriend's hand and pulled him along with her as she hurried toward Courtney and Graham.

He was a handsome kid, and one year older than Rachel. Courtney knew Graham would think his curly brown hair was a little too long, and wouldn't care for the preppy clothes he was wearing. But Courtney also knew Graham had been preppy once upon a time himself, and she would certainly remind her husband of that when he started picking the poor kid apart.

From the hours she'd spent on the phone with Rachel since she left for college in New York, Courtney knew they'd met at Rachel's first ever frat party, and that Rachel had liked him immediately. He'd walked Rachel back to her dorm to make sure she got home safe and that's when he'd asked her out.

Courtney also knew Rachel really liked this boy, though Rachel hadn't told her that. Courtney had heard it in Rachel's voice. Now she could see it on Rachel's face.

"This is Brian," Rachel said, beaming. "Brian, these are my parents, Courtney and Graham."

"Brian Walters. Nice to meet you both," he said, sticking out his hand for Graham to shake.

Graham shook his hand. But Courtney couldn't say he was pleased about it.

"I'll go get your luggage," Graham said, heading toward the end of the dock, where Gil was unloading the suitcases.

"Let me help you with those, sir," Brian called out and hurried after Graham.

"Well?" Rachel demanded.

"He's adorable," Courtney told her.

Rachel looked down the dock in his direction, where Brian and Graham were talking to Gil. "Yes, he is adorable, and I can't wait for Tiki to meet him. She is going to *d-i-e* with envy."

"Don't be so sure about that," Courtney said. "Tiki's bringing a guest to Thanksgiving dinner tomorrow, too. He's from Point Baker. His dad owns the store where Yanoo buys his carving supplies. And Hanya says it's *l-o-v-e*."

Rachel snorted. "Well, it isn't quite to the *l-o-v-e* stage with Brian yet, but it's close."

"How close?"

"Don't worry," Rachel said and grinned. "Brian's a good guy like Dad."

That made Courtney smile, too.

Until Rachel's eyes dropped to Courtney's stomach.

"You are *huge,*" Rachel said, pulling Courtney's sweater open to get a better look.

Courtney put both hands on her round belly. "I am not *huge.* I weigh exactly what I should weigh at six months."

"But you are still going to come back to civilization to give birth to my baby brother, right?"

"Yes," Courtney said. "Beth and my mother would kill me if I didn't."

"Beth is way too cool," Rachel said. "But I'll never forget the look on your mother's face when she came riding up to the gazebo in Hal's skiff. She looked as if she'd just landed on Mars."

They both laughed.

As Graham had predicted, his parents hadn't attended their wedding. But they'd thrown them a huge reception when they came to New York for Christmas that year, the same year Rachel started her junior year in high school in Anchorage.

"How are your grandparents? Are you still seeing them all on a regular basis?"

"My mother's parents are in Greece and won't be back until sometime next spring. But Gram Morrison took me shopping the other day while Gramps was playing golf, and she bought me those boots I wanted, so cross those off my Christmas list."

"Will do," Courtney said. "I'm just glad we're coming to New York for Christmas this year. That means you can go to some of the Lamaze classes with me."

"Ewwww," Rachel said, "I don't think so." But she did reach out and give a quick pat to Courtney's stomach. "Sorry, Jonah. If there's any deep breathing going on, it's going to be mine."

"Rachel!" Courtney scolded, but she had to laugh.

"Of course, you know when Jonah hits thirteen and realizes what he's missing stuck out here in nowhere land, he isn't going to be thrilled about it any more than I was. And that's when my little brother can come to

New York and live with his cool big sister who will show him how the real world lives."

"Did you hear that, Graham?" Courtney called out.

Graham and Brian walked up beside them, each carrying two suitcases. "Did I hear what?"

"Rachel just told me that when Jonah turns thirteen and starts being a real pain-in-the-butt teenager, he can go to New York and live with his cool big sister."

Graham looked over at Rachel. "Can we have that in writing?"

Rachel rolled her eyes.

Courtney laughed.

Broadway barked and wagged his tail.

But as Rachel ran ahead with Brian, eager to show him the lodge, Courtney knew something Rachel wasn't old enough to realize yet. She knew that regardless of Rachel's insistence that she was too cool for a place like Port Protection, this was a place Rachel would return to with her children someday.

A place where troubles melted away. Where living in such an unspoiled environment had the ability to renew your spirit, give you strength and remind you of how truly remarkable God's gifts to man really are. And where standing on the deck at first light, watching the fog roll across the cove, made everything right in your world.

When she came, Courtney and Graham would be waiting.

Willing to share such an amazing experience.

* * * * *

Harlequin Intrigue top author
Delores Fossen presents
a brand-new series
of breathtaking romantic suspense!
TEXAS MATERNITY: HOSTAGES
The first installment available May 2010:
THE BABY'S GUARDIAN

Shaw cursed and hooked his arm around Sabrina.

Despite the urgency that the deadly gunfire created, he tried to be careful with her, and he took the brunt of the fall when he pulled her to the ground. His shoulder hit hard, but he held on tight to his gun so that it wouldn't be jarred from his hand.

Shaw didn't stop there. He crawled over Sabrina, sheltering her pregnant belly with his body, and he came up ready to return fire.

This was obviously a situation he'd wanted to avoid at all cost. He didn't want his baby in the middle of a fight with these armed fugitives, but when they fired that shot, they'd left him no choice. Now, the trick was to get Sabrina safely out of there.

"Get down," someone on the SWAT team yelled from the roof of the adjacent building.

Shaw did. He dropped lower, covering Sabrina as best he could.

There was another shot, but this one came from a rifleman on the SWAT team. Shaw didn't look up, but he heard the sound of glass being blown apart.

The shots continued, all coming from his men, which

meant it might be time to try to get Sabrina to better cover. Shaw glanced at the front of the building.

So that Sabrina's pregnant belly wouldn't be smashed against the ground, Shaw eased off her and moved her to a sitting position so that her back was against the brick wall. They were close. Too close. And face-to-face.

He found himself staring right into those sea-green eyes.

How will Shaw get Sabrina out?
Follow the daring rescue and the heartbreaking aftermath in THE BABY'S GUARDIAN
by Delores Fossen,
available May 2010 from Harlequin Intrigue.